2x 1/22 c+. 19/18

The Showstopper

A Rebecca Mystery

by Mary Casanova

✩ American Girl®

americangirl.com/service

For Lucia,
and all who love the stage

Beforever™

The adventurous characters you'll meet in
the BeForever books will spark your curiosity
about the past, inspire you to find your voice
in the present, and excite you about your future.
You'll make friends with these girls as you share
their fun and their challenges. Like you, they are
bright and brave, imaginative and energetic,
creative and kind. Just as you are, they are
discovering what really matters: Helping others.
Being a true friend. Protecting the earth.
Standing up for what's right. Read their stories,
explore their worlds, join their adventures.
Your friendship with them will BeForever.

TABLE *of* CONTENTS

chapter 1

Stagestruck

"THANK GOODNESS YOUR brother saved us!" Rebecca said. Arm in arm with her cousin, Ana, the two girls climbed the stairs from the subway station. "I'd much rather visit a theater on Broadway than stay home embroidering doilies with our grandmother on such a warm day."

Ana giggled, and then turned serious, adjusting her grip on the lunch basket she carried. "Yes, but is not good Michael forgot his lunch," she said in her thick Russian accent. "With both Papa and my brother Josef out of work, my family needs money Michael will earn. How can he be hard worker if he has no food?"

"True," Rebecca agreed. "He's lucky he has us—and *we're* lucky he forgot his lunch or else we'd still be at home pricking our fingers with our embroidery needles!"

"But Bubbie would be happy if we do needle-work!" Ana teased.

"And *we* would be miserable!" Rebecca replied, throwing her arm over her forehead dramatically and making her cousin laugh.

The midday sun pierced Rebecca's eyes. She stepped out of the flow of people to get her bearings and check the street signs. They'd made their route from the Lower East Side to 42nd Street, close to Times Square and Broadway. "We're right where we should be. The Victory Theater is only a half block away!"

The sidewalk and street bustled with pushcarts and vendors selling fresh flowers, fruit, and tickets to Broadway shows. She and Ana wove past a group of ladies whose hair was tucked under fashionable hats and whose tight-waisted dresses skimmed their ankles. A boy wearing suspenders and a jaunty cap hawked newspapers at the corner. Businessmen whisked by in well-pressed suits and polished shoes.

"Ana, look!" Rebecca said, pointing. Towering four stories above them, the Victory Theater proclaimed its presence with huge letters along its rooftop. "That's it!"

"Michael works *there*?" Ana said with awe.

Rebecca grinned and started toward the theater.

"Wait!" Ana stopped under the marquee of a neighboring theater. She pointed at a poster featuring the image of a young starlet with captivating eyes set in a heart-shaped face. Auburn curls framed her flawless skin and demure smile.

"I know her!" Ana exclaimed.

"All of New York knows her!" Rebecca said. She read the poster aloud:

> THE PRETTIEST SHOPGIRL IN NEW YORK
> OLIVIA BERRY
> TO TAKE THE STAGE WITH
> THE FAMOUS ZIEGFELD FOLLIES
> AT THE NEW AMSTERDAM THEATER!

Oh! Rebecca dreamed of being a famous actress. And here was Olivia Berry—who just last spring was an ordinary girl working in a shop—with a show of her own. *Such luck!*

Rebecca lingered a second longer, trying not to feel envious. She reminded herself that she'd been lucky, too, when she'd recently gone to watch her mother's cousin Max and his fiancée, Lily, act on a movie set—and stumbled into her own small role in the film! Those brief moments as a real actress had given Rebecca a taste for the stage, and now she wanted more.

Acting here on Broadway would be thrilling, Rebecca thought. On Broadway, unlike in movies, every song, dance, comedy skit, and magic show was performed live, right in front of the audience. Actors didn't get the chance to do a second or third "take" on a scene. They had to get it right the first time, each and every performance. In Rebecca's eyes, being live onstage was as exciting as being in a movie.

It could happen, she told herself. *You never know when another unexpected opportunity might turn up!* With a sigh, she turned away and gazed across the street at the Victory Theater, excitement zipping up her spine. "Let's go!" she said, grabbing Ana's hand.

Eyes open for fresh horse manure, speeding carriages, and honking automobiles, the girls hurried across the street. A white-haired doorman greeted them with a tip of his hat as they stepped up to the ornately carved double doors. "Are you lost, young ladies?"

"We need to deliver lunch to my cousin, Michael Rubin," Rebecca said. "He's a painter here."

"I'll see to it that it gets to him," the doorman replied, reaching for the basket on Ana's arm.

Rebecca thought fast, quickly stepping between the doorman and Ana. She was too close to a real Broadway theater to simply walk away! She longed for a peek at the stage, or a glimpse of a performer or two. "Thank you, sir, but he insisted that we deliver it in person," she explained.

"And why is that?" the man asked, tilting his head.

Rebecca frowned and did her best to look serious. "Well," she replied, "he said he has reason to worry that it may not reach him, and under no circumstances were we to leave this in anyone else's hands but his. We promised!" She dropped her voice. "After all, sir, a promise is a promise."

The doorman let out a long, slow breath, as if he'd heard this excuse before. "The painters are working on the rooftop," he said, holding the door wide. "Take the stairs. The elevator is for patrons."

"Thank you, kind sir!" Rebecca said. She hoped she hadn't been too dramatic.

Ana elbowed her as they stepped inside. "Rebecca!" she whispered. "That wasn't all true."

"Just a little acting, Ana," Rebecca reassured her. "It worked, didn't it?"

The girls headed up the staircase, quickly at first and then slowly after the long climb began to steal

their breath. Just as they rounded the last turn, a
large rat skittered across the landing in front of Ana,
making her jump and nearly drop the lunch basket.
"Oh!" she cried. "I do *not* like rats!"

"Neither do I!" Rebecca answered, shrinking back.
Ignoring the ache in her lungs, Rebecca raced up the
remaining stairs with Ana. They burst through the
door at the top.

Emerging into the bright sunlight, Rebecca caught
her breath and stared, open-mouthed. This was no
ordinary rooftop—it was a whole new world above
the city! To her left, hundreds of seats fanned out in
front of a stage, where acrobats practiced spins and
flips. To the right, Rebecca spotted a flowing creek,
a pond with boats, and what looked like a ruined
castle. Beyond the open-air café at the center of the
huge space, steps rose to an arching wooden bridge
leading to a little farm that looked just like the ones
Rebecca had read about in fairy tales. The barn
looked almost like a house, with dormers and paned

windows. Towering over the farm's green gardens was a Dutch windmill, its sails spinning with a soft *whup, whup, whup.*

"Is this heaven?" Ana said, covering her mouth and holding back a giggle. "Oh my!"

"It's beautiful," Rebecca agreed. She turned toward the stage and was imagining herself there, doing a comedy routine, making an audience laugh, when Michael stepped out from around the stage's backdrop. He took off his painter's hat, exposing his straight brown hair, and waved the cap high above his head.

The girls followed him behind the stage, where a man was painting a scene of white swans amid blooming lily pads on a wooden backdrop. The scene looked so real that Rebecca almost thought she could dive into it. Michael spoke to the painter—a short man with weathered skin and a mop of red curls— before rejoining the girls.

"I ask to take break early. My boss, Mr. O'Hara, I want to keep on good side." Michael laughed. "He is amazing scene painter. He has come far; he is immigrant, like us," he said, nudging Ana. Then he reached for the lunch basket. "I am starving!"

The trio found a patch of shade beneath the huge flowerpots that lined the edge of the rooftop. "Please, share," he said, pulling rye bread, sausage, carrots, and dill pickles from the basket.

Rebecca broke off a small chunk of bread. "You're so lucky to work here!" she said.

"Not as lucky as Mr. O'Hara." Michael held up his hand, fingers splayed. "He start here just five months ago. He work hard, and already is boss, called 'head set painter.' In America, you can be anything!" He grinned and took a bite of sausage.

"Take your time eating, Michael," Rebecca said, enraptured by it all. "I want to stay here as long as possible." She ventured closer to the railing at the edge of the rooftop and risked a glance toward the street, but it was such a long way down that it made her insides spin, and she looked away. Just as she sat down again, the nearby elevator doors opened.

A tall, square-shouldered man stepped out. Despite the heat, he wore a black vest, black coat with tails, and a towering top hat. He strode down the theater aisle and talked with the acrobat troupe onstage.

"That is Mr. Oscar Hammerstein," Michael said. "He owns whole building and runs the theater. He hired me."

Soon Mr. Hammerstein was headed in their direction, squinting curiously at Rebecca and Ana. "Girls, where are your parents?"

Michael jumped up and wiped his hands on his paint-splattered overalls. "Sorry, Mr. Hammerstein," he said. "I forget lunch, and my sister and cousin, they bring to me."

Mr. Hammerstein crossed his arms and studied the girls. Though his stare made Rebecca squirm, she held her head high and smiled back. *This man owns the whole theater!* she thought. *This could be one of those unexpected opportunities.*

"You," he said to Rebecca finally. "You would be perfect for a supporting role here on the rooftop."

"Really?" Rebecca held her breath. A thrill of anticipation bubbled up inside her.

Mr. Hammerstein looked to Ana. "Both of you. In fact, you can start tomorrow morning. Mind you, payday doesn't come until the end of the week."

"But tomorrow's the Sabbath," Ana said. "We're Jewish."

Rebecca shot her cousin a silencing stare. Yes, Saturdays were traditionally the day of rest for Jewish families. But things in America were different from Russia, where her cousins used to live, and *this* looked like a huge opportunity. Why ruin it before they even knew what it was?

Mr. Hammerstein harrumphed. "Well I'm Jewish, too, but that's never stopped me from conducting business. I say treat every day like it's the opening night of the performance."

Rebecca nodded. "My father keeps our shoe

shop open on Saturdays. I've worked many times with him when he's needed help."

Mr. Hammerstein nodded. "See? Good Jewish girls can certainly work on the Sabbath."

"I'm sure my parents will let us come back tomorrow," Rebecca declared. In truth, she wasn't at all sure her parents—or Ana's—would allow them to play parts on a vaudeville stage. *Still,* she thought, *if you don't act confident, you don't get the part.*

"Then you must get measured for costumes before you leave," Mr. Hammerstein insisted. "You'll find our seamstress, Mrs. Rothstein, on the third floor."

"See you in the morning!" Rebecca said as Mr. Hammerstein turned and walked away.

"Rebecca!" Ana frowned. "I know you want to be actress. And I want job, too, to help my family. But you should not promise. We must ask parents first!"

Rebecca met her eyes. "Don't worry, Ana. It can't hurt to act hopeful."

...

"Watch for rats," Ana warned as they entered the stairwell again.

Rebecca shuddered, and they hurried down two flights to the costume shop on the third floor. Squeezing between racks of dresses covered in ruffles, lace, and sequins, the girls made their way to the fitting area. They passed a cutting table laden with bolts of sheer cloth and silky ribbon, and Rebecca couldn't help running her fingers along the satiny fabrics. The costumes were as colorful as candy, she thought, and a hundred times more beautiful.

They found tiny Mrs. Rothstein in the center of it all, stitching the sleeves of a feathery jacket.

Rebecca greeted her. "Mr. Hammerstein said that he had supporting roles for us," she explained proudly.

"Sit," Mrs. Rothstein said, speaking around the pins she held between her lips. "You girls are not so important. I have other acts that come before you."

Rebecca and Ana shared an amused look and sat down on a velvet couch in the corner. At last, the tiny woman set down the jacket and eyed the cousins from head to toe. Then she draped each girl with fabric and set about measuring and marking at expert speed. "Yes, good. Very good," she said as she worked, her hands and body in constant motion. "Stand straight," she told Rebecca, who was practically vibrating with excitement. "There. Good. Done."

By the time Rebecca and Ana reached the lobby, Michael was waiting for them. Once the three of them were on the subway, Rebecca plopped on a seat beside Michael and Ana and sighed happily.

"I can't believe this!" she said. "What do you suppose we'll do onstage? Ana and I performed at the school assembly, so we've had practice singing, but perhaps we'll have to learn to dance." Rebecca paused for a moment. "Maybe we'll need to audition so they can decide which roles we get."

"If Hammerstein wants you in show," Michael said with admiration, "he make it happen like Houdini. But convincing our parents not so easy."

Rebecca turned to Ana. "We'll talk to them during dinner tonight," she declared. "But how will we persuade them?"

"We tell first about payment," Ana suggested.

Rebecca nodded. "Good thinking. Keep it practical. Jobs and money."

Michael lifted his forefinger in warning. "You girls be careful. Mr. Hammerstein, he not so honest, I am told."

"Oh?" Rebecca said, not eager to hear anything that might dampen her hopes.

"I hear he fill whole Victory building with stolen goods. When big passenger ship stuck in harbor, Mr. Hammerstein, he find out and steal every rug, every furniture from ship for his theaters. What they call this, funny word ... *flimflammery*?"

"Flimflum-what?" Ana asked.

"Flimflam. A kind of trick, I think," Rebecca replied.

"It's like this," Michael said. He pulled a penny from the pocket of his overalls and held it up. "Let's say you give me penny." He closed his fist around the coin, made a rolling motion with his hands, and opened his fist again. The penny was gone! He opened his other hand, and there it was.

The girls laughed.

"If I make your penny disappear and give it back to you, what you call that?" he asked.

"Magic trick," Ana said, beaming.

Michael did the trick again. This time, both palms were empty. "But if I make your coin disappear and you never see it again, what you call that?"

"Cheat," Ana answered.

"Swindle," Rebecca said. *"Flimflam."*

Michael nodded. He reached into his pocket, pulled out the missing penny, and held it up. "I think Mr. Hammerstein like to keep other people's money in his pocket. Believe me, I'm happy for job. But I feel better when he pay me the money."

Rebecca crossed her arms and whispered. "Michael, would you mind not saying anything about flimflams to our parents? This could *still* be a great chance for Ana and me to get onstage."

"Sure," Michael said. "But if you get job, I say, keep one eye open."

chapter 2

Surprise!

REBECCA LOVED THE Sabbath, which
began with a traditional family meal every Friday
night. When the cousins arrived home, the table
was set for dinner, and the two candles in their
heavy Shabbat candlesticks waited to be lit. Mama
was wrapping freshly baked challah in a cloth, and
the braided loaves of bread filled the kitchen with a
sweet, yeasty fragrance. Rebecca wanted a slice that
very moment, but she knew that she must wait until
dinner, when a prayer would be recited just before
the loaves were cut.

A knock came on the apartment door. Rebecca
ran to open it. To her delight, Max and Lily stepped
inside.

"Room for two more?" Lily said, flashing Rebecca

a smile and planting a kiss on her cheek.

"Of course!" Papa replied. "Shabbat is for family."

As the family moved their chairs closer to make room for the latecomers and Mama bustled about adding extra plates, Max threw his arm around Rebecca's shoulders. "I heard about the strike and your brave speech." Then he whispered in Rebecca's ear, "Those acting skills come in handy, don't they?"

Rebecca nodded, her cheeks growing warm. When she'd written a letter to the newspaper weeks ago, complaining about conditions at the clothing factory where her uncle worked, she'd never dreamed she'd end up reading it aloud to a large group of protesting factory employees. She'd acted confident and used a brave voice, despite feeling scared. She'd mustered that same confidence today at the Victory, hoping it might lead to new opportunities. She wanted to tell Max all about Mr. Hammerstein and the acting job, but she knew this wasn't the time.

The dinner table overflowed with Papa, Mama,

Rebecca's twin older sisters, her brothers, Bubbie and Grandpa, Ana's family, and now Max and Lily. Rebecca lit the candles, Papa prayed a blessing, and then everyone sang "Shalom Aleichem," a song about welcoming angels of peace into the home. Rebecca smiled. It was as if God had sent her angels in the form of Max and Lily. *Who better to help make her case for acting roles at Hammerstein's theater than two film stars?*

Through dinner, Rebecca couldn't stop picturing herself on the rooftop stage. When she could eat no more and could no longer concentrate on the dinner conversation, she jumped in. "Mama? Papa?"

"What is it, Rebecca?" Papa said. Suddenly everyone fell silent as they turned their eyes to her. Rebecca glanced at Ana, who gave her an encouraging nod.

Rebecca took a deep breath and pushed ahead. "Ana and I were measured for costumes today at the Victory Theater, where Michael works."

"Costumes? Whatever for?" Mama said, eyeing Rebecca with curiosity.

"We've been offered supporting roles onstage," Rebecca said. "We're even going to be paid for our work!"

Mama's gaze flickered over to Michael, who didn't say a word, much to Rebecca's relief.

Ana and I are at least as sure about receiving payment as Michael is, she reasoned. The term *flimflam* fluttered through her mind, and she willed it to fly on by before turning back to her parents and pressing on. "The only thing we need, of course, is your permission."

She didn't realize how much she had been holding inside until she exhaled loudly. *There.* She'd said it.

She glanced at Max, who winked at her, as if reminding her that some things were still secret— like the film she'd played a part in, which was yet to be released. He rested his hand on top of Lily's.

Bubbie, her gray wig slightly askew, didn't hide

her feelings. "Those Ziegfeld Girls who dance in their underwear and stockings—is scandalous!"

"Bubbie," Max said, "not all roles on Broadway or in film are scandalous. Besides, the Ziegfeld Follies are in a different theater across the street from the Victory. Beckie and Ana aren't being asked to be in the Follies, right?" He looked to Rebecca.

Grateful for his help, she smiled. "No, a supporting role in . . . comedy acts, skits, maybe some singing—"

"Vaudeville." Bubbie spat out the word.

Max leaned back in his chair. "There are respectable acts even in vaudeville. It's not the same as performing in a Broadway musical or playing a part for the films, but it could be a start. A place to practice acting skills."

Rebecca shot Cousin Max an appreciative grin, and then turned her gaze to Mama and Papa. "Mr. Oscar Hammerstein himself sent us to be measured for costumes. He told us we could start work tomorrow," she said. "It would be such a shame if the seamstress did all that work for nothing."

"Girls," Uncle Jacob said. "You know the Sabbath is day of rest."

Ana nodded and finally chimed in. "Yes, Papa," she said, "but we need money. And Michael already is working so hard."

Rebecca nodded. "Just until Uncle Jacob and Josef find jobs," she chimed in. "Every dollar we make will go to help Ana and her family."

Bubbie pondered this for a moment. "I don't like you work on Sabbath. But Ana's family in such hard time now." She looked to Michael. "You can look out for girls there?"

Michael nodded. "Yes. The girls can come and go with me. I make sure that nothing bad happen."

Rebecca's hopes rose as Bubbie looked to Papa. Papa and Mama looked to Ana's parents.

Things are turning in our favor, Rebecca thought as she and Ana shared a hopeful glance. *The less I say, the better.*

...

Pausing beneath the gilded lampposts outside the Victory the next morning, Rebecca gripped Ana's hand. "Let's stop for a minute," she said. "For our first rehearsal, we want to look calm and confident, not rushed."

"Take your time," Michael said, walking ahead, "but I need to get to work."

"If there's an audition," Rebecca mused, "I could do something funny like I did on Coney Island. Or I could recite the speech I made at the strike site— standing up for the fair treatment of workers."

"Maybe I sing song from spring recital," said Ana.

They met each other's eyes and shared a grin.

"I still can't believe we got permission to come back!" Rebecca said.

"If . . ." Ana reminded her.

Rebecca nodded. "Yes, *if.*"

There were a lot of *ifs.* Their parents had agreed

that Rebecca and Ana could return to Hammerstein's theater, but only *if* Michael agreed that the roles were respectable for young girls. And they could work *only until* Uncle Jacob and Josef found work—or until school started in two weeks.

Rebecca drew in a gulp of warm city air. "Let's go."

Then the girls walked through the doors and up the stairs to try on their new costumes.

"I worked all night," Mrs. Rothstein said, removing two blue outfits from a rack. She pointed to two dressing rooms. "Try them on."

A few moments later, the girls stepped out in identical white blouses with puffed short sleeves, lightweight blue overalls, and long cotton stockings. Rebecca curtsied to her reflection in the full-length mirror. "Our costumes are adorable!" she said. "Even Bubbie would approve. Nothing scandalous!"

Mrs. Rothstein handed them each a pair of knee-high rubber boots. "Not easy finding sizes for you, but here you are."

Boots? Rebecca's smile shrank the slightest bit. The tall black boots were not pretty, and certainly not good for dancing. But, she thought, perhaps the costume was for a comedy routine. Boots like that could be funny, at least, even if they weren't glamorous.

She pulled on the boots. They fit perfectly.

Mrs. Rothstein gave the girls an approving nod. "Okay. Now, up to the top with you!"

"Thank you, Mrs. Rothstein!" Rebecca wanted to hug her. As she and Ana climbed the stairs, she practically skipped from step to step, forgetting even to watch out for rats. *To the top!* she told herself. *We are on our way to the top!*

Emerging from the stairway, Rebecca looked for Mr. Hammerstein, or someone who looked like a stage director, until a woman waving from outside the barn caught her eye.

"Over here, girls!" the woman called. Her white

puff-sleeve blouse, red corset-style bodice, blue skirt, and white apron showed off an hourglass figure. "Mr. Hammerstein told me to expect you!" She waved them closer.

As they walked toward the barn, Rebecca looked back across the expanse of empty seats to the stage. "Mr. Hammerstein offered us supporting roles in the theater. Shouldn't we be over there?"

The woman's laugh was high and breezy. "Well, you've got 'supporting roles' all right! You're just where you're supposed to be. I'm Flora. What are your names?"

"Rebecca Rubin. But my friends call me Beckie."

"I'm Ana Rubin."

"Sisters," Flora said.

"Cousins," Ana corrected her.

Flora took a moment to study the girls from their boots to the crown of their heads. "You look perfect," she said. "The question is, are you serious about chores? I can't do all the farmwork myself."

Chores? As Ana nodded, Rebecca could only look down at her clunky rubber boots. She had a sudden feeling they had made a terrible mistake.

"Do you like farm animals?" Flora continued.

Ana's face lit up. "I love all animals!" she said, then her face grew serious. "Except rats. I am very frightened of rats."

"Don't worry," Flora said soothingly. "You won't be in charge of any rats here." She put her hand on Ana's shoulder. "You have a sweet accent. Where are you from?"

"Russia," Ana said, her smile widening. "We do not have farms on rooftops in Russia."

Flora laughed. "No, I suppose not. It's unusual, even for New York City!"

"But I thought ..." Rebecca began. She swallowed past a growing lump of disappointment and tried again. "I thought we were going to be onstage."

Flora put her hands on her hips. "Everything's a stage here, Beckie. This farm is a kind of theater.

Customers come for the shows, food, and drink. That's where I come in. They love to watch a Dutch maid milk the cow. I give them milk fresh from the bucket. They bring their children and spend hours enjoying this little piece of heaven on a summer evening. And it is your job to keep the farm tidy and in working order so that they may enjoy it."

Rebecca's heart slid down a few notches. There would be, she realized, no singing or dancing, no comedy routines—only buckets and boots and boring chores. "I think there's been some mistake," she blurted, holding back tears. "I'd better talk to Mr. Hammerstein."

"No point in that," Flora said matter-of-factly. "We may not be the Ziegfeld Follies, but we are one of the most popular stops in the city. If you want a job, this is it. Take it or leave it."

"We take it," Ana said enthusiastically before Rebecca could respond.

Flora smiled. "Good. I'll show you around."

Rebecca trudged behind Ana as Flora led them through the barn, past animal pens, and alongside one of the vegetable gardens. Their work, Flora told the girls, would consist of cleaning stalls, washing out milk buckets, pulling weeds, keeping goats brushed, and making sure everything was "shipshape" before the customers arrived. When they returned to the barn, she handed each girl a broom.

"May as well get started," she said brightly.

Outside the barn, Rebecca flicked her broom halfheartedly at a small clump of hay. She was working up the courage to tell Flora she was quitting when she spotted a lovely young woman approaching. The woman's dress had so many layers of soft green fabric that it made a gentle swishing noise as she came closer.

"Gee," the woman said. "You look like you could be my little sister!"

"I do?" Rebecca gazed up at the woman's heart-shaped face and the soft tendrils of auburn hair escaping from beneath her wide-brimmed hat.

That face! Rebecca would know it anywhere. "You're Olivia Berry!" she gasped. "Prettiest Shopgirl in New York City!"

"Shhh," the woman said, holding a finger to her perfectly painted lips. "Call me Ollie."

Rebecca introduced herself and Ana. Ollie smiled, and Rebecca understood instantly why Olivia Berry had won the contest. She was pretty in a way that somehow made you feel as if you'd been friends forever and ever.

"I'm here for my daily glass of fresh milk—for my complexion," Ollie said, pressing her palm to her cheek theatrically. "It's all the rage, you know."

Rebecca nodded, mesmerized. "I'm not sure where . . ." she began. Flora had said something earlier about fresh milk, and Rebecca suddenly wished she'd been paying more attention.

"We are new here," Ana explained.

"Follow me, girls," Ollie said.

Rebecca and Ana put down their brooms and

trailed behind her. Just then, Michael's boss, Mr. O'Hara, appeared around the corner of the barn, adjusting the collar of his paint-splattered work shirt.

"Good morning, Miss Olivia!" he said.

"Good morning," Ollie answered without even turning in his direction.

Mr. O'Hara continued in a lilting voice:

> *"'Go and love, go and love, young man,*
> *If the lady be young and fair.'*
> *Ay, penny, brown penny, brown penny,*
> *I am looped in the loops of her hair."*

Rebecca recognized the lines. Her teacher last year had loved to read poetry by William Butler Yeats. Mr. O'Hara's singsong accent made the poem sound even more beautiful, she thought.

"Lovely, Mr. O'Hara," Ollie said, not breaking her stride. It didn't seem to Rebecca that she meant it.

With a flourish, Mr. O'Hara opened the door and

bowed his head of red curls as Ollie passed, as if she were a queen. As he did so, a metal flask dropped to his feet. *Thunk.* Mr. O'Hara swept up the flask and sheepishly stashed it back in his shirt pocket as Ollie fluttered past him.

"You've not seen that, girls," he whispered. Then he gave Rebecca a wink.

Rebecca looked away quickly. She was pretty sure that flasks like that were used for carrying whiskey and other strong drinks. Was Mr. O'Hara drinking on the job? She heard Bubbie's disapproving voice in her head, and wondered for a moment if she should tell Michael. But as she hurried behind Ollie into the barn, she swiftly dismissed the thought. Telling Michael about Mr. O'Hara's flask might make Michael decide their job was unsuitable for young girls. And thanks to Miss Olivia Berry, the job suddenly seemed *much* more interesting.

Inside the barn, a sweet aroma rose from the hay bales stacked against the wall. On the opposite wall, a row of low windows cast soft light onto a wide ceramic sink, counter, cabinet, and icebox.

"Hello, Flora," Olivia said, her voice cheerful. "I'm here for my milk."

"Hello, Ollie," Flora said, rising from a wooden bench. She opened the icebox, and cold air rushed out. Six pitchers of milk filled the shelves. Flora withdrew a pitcher, filled a glass from the cabinet, and handed the milk to Ollie.

"I see you have new helpers," Ollie said. "That's perfect, because now that the Follies are in rehearsal every day, I won't have time to come for my milk myself. I'll need someone to deliver it to my dressing room at the New Amsterdam."

"I could do that," Rebecca offered quickly. If she couldn't be onstage, getting closer to a famous performer would be the next best thing. And the Follies were just across the street, Max had said.

"Oh, Beckie, I'd be ever so grateful," Ollie said, clapping her hands together. Then she sighed dramatically. "I'm so dreadfully busy learning dance steps for the Follies. Stage life is leaving me utterly exhausted!"

Flora rolled her eyes. "Such problems! Can't someone from your own theater get the milk for you?"

"Sadly, there's really no one at the Amsterdam I can ask," Ollie said. "I haven't made many friends yet among the Ziegfeld Girls. It's . . . it's very competitive. I've got my first big role in the new show, and there's a lot riding on my performance. If the show's a success, the sky's the limit for me. If it's not . . ." Ollie straightened her shoulders. "Well, I just won't think about that. I've come too far to go back to waiting on customers in a shop."

Ollie sighed again. "I could use some help—just until the new show opens on Friday. Is that too much to ask?"

"I suppose not," Flora managed.

"Well, it's settled then!" Ollie drank her milk, licked her rosebud lips, and set the glass on the countertop. "I'll let the doorman know to expect Beckie at lunch. As Flora well knows, our doorman, Mr. Teller, is a tough nut to crack," she said. "He has a difficult job. He's always turning away men who claim to be madly in love with one of us Ziegfeld Girls. I swear, they come around like bees to honey!"

"I'm sure they do," Flora said, her tone sour.

Rebecca's thoughts bounced to Mr. O'Hara. She had wondered why Ollie had been so cool toward him, but now she supposed that with so many people wanting your attention, it might be hard to show your appreciation for everyone—even if they recited poetry for you.

Ollie suddenly squinted at Rebecca, breaking her train of thought. "Hey," she said, "you look so much like my sister that I think you could pass in and out quite easily!" She patted her tiny green purse. "I'm able to pay, of course—sis. See you tomorrow then?" Her smile was like a warm hug, inviting Rebecca into her world.

Then with a swish of gauzy fabric, Ollie was gone.

Flora snorted. "She thinks the world revolves around her."

Mr. O'Hara stepped into the barn. It was clear to Rebecca that he had been waiting outside, hoping for another glimpse of Ollie. "Flora," he said, "you're jealous. I'll admit, that ethereal creature takes me breath away."

Ana's brow wrinkled. "What's *ethereal*?" she asked.

Flora shrugged. "Beats me. Our dear Mr. O'Hara is always spouting fancy words and poetry. I think he makes half of it up!" She smiled a teasing smile, as if they shared a private joke.

Mr. O'Hara closed his eyes and grinned. "Ah, *ethereal* ... means she's so entirely perfect, so delicate, that she's barely of this world."

"You've lost your mind, Mr. O'Hara," Flora said. "I knew Ollie before she was famous. We worked at the same department store. Just a regular gal. In fact, if I hadn't told her about that 'prettiest shopgirl' contest, she wouldn't be where she is today."

"On that, we disagree," Mr. O'Hara said. "Heaven sent, she is."

Rebecca couldn't help nodding. To her, Ollie really was heavenly, and it didn't seem right that Flora, and the performers who shared the stage with Ollie, couldn't see that. Still, Rebecca knew from her brief time on the film set with Max and Lily that actors could be fiercely competitive. Everyone wanted to reach the top—and there were only a few spotlight roles. How awful to work in a place where no one would be happy for your success! Rebecca suddenly felt protective toward Ollie.

"I can't wait until our lunch break tomorrow—" she started.

Irritation flared in Flora's eyes. "Girls, you work for me, but Mr. Hammerstein is the one who pays you. You must clear this with him first—*after* you've put in a full day's work."

The girls nodded, surprised at Flora's sudden

crossness, and left the barn to continue their work.

As she swept, Rebecca's broom felt as light as a feather. With any luck, by this time tomorrow, she would see where Ollie and the Ziegfeld Girls performed. If only Mr. Hammerstein would agree!

chapter 3

A Strange Request

THAT AFTERNOON, REBECCA put all
her energy into playing the part of a perfectly happy
farm girl. As she raked the chicken yard, a small
orchestra onstage was practicing "The Little Ford
Rambled Right Along." The song had honking noises
that made Rebecca giggle, and as she hoed between
rows of beans, squash, and peppers, she couldn't
help singing along. At the end of each row, she took
a twirl, pretending to dance with a partner. When
the song ended, she stopped and fanned herself. That
part wasn't an act—being a farm girl was hard work.
Even so, Rebecca thought, if it gave her the chance to
deepen a friendship with Olivia Berry and see the
famous Ziegfeld Follies behind the scenes, it would
all be worth it.

When Flora gave the girls another chore inside the barn, Rebecca sighed with relief. It would be cooler out of the sun. "Parents won't bring their children to watch me milk the cows if the stalls aren't clean," Flora said. "Every day, you must shovel them out, put lime on the wet spots, and fill the stalls with clean straw."

"Lime?" Ana asked. "Like lemon? This is strange custom."

Flora's laugh was musical. "Not *that* kind of lime," she said. "Here, I'll show you."

She removed the top of a wooden barrel and filled a metal scoop with white powder. "This is lime. It gets rid of that nose-pinching smell."

Ana lowered her gaze to the floor. "I didn't know this word has more than one meaning."

Flora put her fingers under Ana's chin and lifted it until their eyes met. "Don't be embarrassed. You speak two languages. I only know English. Besides, your accent is adorable!"

Ana's pink cheeks deepened in color, and as she

smiled back at Flora, Rebecca suddenly felt outside the circle of a new friendship. Usually, she was quicker to make friends than shy Ana. But as she shoveled manure into a waiting wheelbarrow, she told herself it really shouldn't bother her. If Mr. Hammerstein gave his permission, she was going to make friends with an up-and-coming Ziegfeld Girl!

When the wheelbarrow was full, the girls took turns pushing it along one of the winding paths toward the manure pile. Along the way, they passed a young man and woman rowing a small boat around the pond, and three young women working in a garden just beyond a group of small stone cottages. Along with woven floppy hats, the women wore blue overalls and white blouses. One of them looked up and waved enthusiastically at Rebecca and Ana as if they were lifelong friends. The girls waved back.

"The same costumes," Ana whispered.

"It really is like playing a part onstage," Rebecca said, wiping stinging sweat from her eyes. The thought made her feel a little better, and the good feeling stayed with her even as they struggled to empty the wheelbarrow into the manure pile.

On their return to the barn, customers were just beginning to arrive. Ladies in pastel dresses stepped off the elevator and opened their parasols. Their children looked freshly scrubbed, their cheeks pink and their clothes spotless.

Rebecca glanced down at her overalls and at Ana's, both now spotted with muck. She held her head high and forced a look of contentment as they pushed the empty wheelbarrow to the barn.

Flora met them at the open door. "Oh, you two are so much more helpful than the other farm girls. They think they're just part of the scenery. They forget that they actually need to work. Thank you, girls! You can talk to Mr. Hammerstein now. His office is on the first floor."

...

As the girls entered his office, Mr. Hammerstein glowered at them from behind an enormous wooden desk. Rebecca coughed, as if to break free the question that suddenly felt stuck in her throat. "Excuse us, Mr. Hammerstein, but we need to ask you something very important."

"So, ask," Mr. Hammerstein said.

"It's about one of your customers." Rebecca explained Ollie's request that she deliver a glass of fresh milk to the neighboring theater during their lunch break each day.

Mr. Hammerstein harrumphed. "That's not what I am paying you for. Those Ziegfeld Girls are awfully high-minded, thinking they can get special deliveries on my dime. Absolutely not. Now go. And close the door behind you."

Rebecca's shoulders sank. "But . . ." She scrambled to come up with another way to ask the question— a way that might lead to yes instead of no. A way that would allow her to salvage the one good thing she'd found in this awful new job. But nothing came to mind. *Mr. Hammerstein doesn't seem like the kind of person you can convince,* Rebecca thought, *not once his mind is made up.* Crushed, she took Ana's hand and turned to go. On the way out, she let the door slam harder than she meant to.

"I guess I'll have to find a way to tell Ollie," Rebecca said as they started down the hall.

"Girls!" Mr. Hammerstein bellowed from behind the closed door. "Come back!"

"We are in trouble?" Ana asked, suddenly looking very worried.

"I don't know," Rebecca said. She turned the doorknob and stepped back in, bracing herself for a scolding.

Mr. Hammerstein was leaning forward on his desk, a freshly lit cigar between his fingers. "New thought," he said. "A unique opportunity. It's always good to keep an eye on the competition." He flicked a bit of ash into a gold-embossed glass ashtray. "My biggest competition is Ziggy Ziegfeld and his blasted New Amsterdam Theater. No matter what I do, he's always trying to one-up me. So, I tell you what. I'll let you make your deliveries to Miss Berry if you—and I mean both of you—fill me in on what's going on over there."

"Both of us?" Ana asked. "But Miss Berry did not say—"

"I need as many eyes and ears on that place as possible," Mr. Hammerstein cut in. "I want to know who's onstage, what's being practiced. I want to know what acts are coming before the public knows."

"You want us to spy," Ana said, crossing her arms over her chest. "In Russia there were spies."

Rebecca stepped on the toe of Ana's boot. Was she trying to ruin everything?

"I wouldn't use that word," Mr. Hammerstein said, taking a puff on his cigar. A cloud of smoke drifted in front of his face. "This is Broadway! I'm simply asking you to be my eyes and ears. Use some acting skills!"

Rebecca liked the word *acting* much better than *spying*.

"One more thought," Mr. Hammerstein continued, leaning across the desk toward them. "I can fill *your* jobs—as well as a certain set painter's position—at any hour of any day. In this city, there's always someone looking for work."

The girls looked at each other, sharing the same thought: He'd backed them into a corner. He was threatening their jobs—and Michael's—if they didn't agree. With Uncle Jacob and Cousin Josef suddenly out of work, Rebecca knew that Michael's job was critical to Ana's family.

Still, Rebecca allowed herself to smile. Mr. Hammerstein may have given them no choice—but he'd also given his approval. Tomorrow they would visit the famous Olivia Berry at the New Amsterdam Theater, and Rebecca couldn't be more excited. "You can rely on us, sir," she said.

"Good," he said. "I'll let Flora know that I have

given permission for both of you to assist Miss Berry. I want you to take a full half hour every day for your delivery. Of course, that means you'll have to work extra hard to get your work done at the farm."

"A half hour?" It was even more than Rebecca had hoped for. "What if we get kicked out of the theater?"

"Act like you belong," he said, "and everyone will assume you do." Then he waved them out the door.

The subway train bounced along, careening around corners and squeaking at each stop. Smelling of the turpentine he'd used to clean paintbrushes, Michael sat by himself. The girls huddled together, going over their day.

"I can't wait to find out more about the *ethereal* Olivia Berry," Rebecca said. "I mean, she's the biggest rising star in all of New York City, and yet she's friendly to us."

"To *you*," Ana corrected her.

Is Ana envious? Rebecca wondered. Remembering how it had stung to feel left out by Flora and Ana earlier in the day, Rebecca tried to smooth things over. "Won't it be fun for us to see what the Follies are all about?" she asked. "Mr. Hammerstein didn't have to ask me to keep my eyes and ears open. I would anyway!"

"Mr. Hammerstein wants us to spy. Nothing good comes of spying," Ana said, gazing out the window at the dark subway walls as they flew past. "We must tell parents."

"No!" Rebecca practically shouted, then softened her voice. "Ana, please. They might not let us keep our jobs. Besides, they don't understand show business. *We* don't understand show business. This is probably how it works."

Ana turned, her eyes somber. "I do not like how it works. If we say no, Michael loses job. We lose job with Flora." She blinked back the start of tears. "My family needs money. And I like Flora."

"That's why we have to keep this to ourselves," Rebecca insisted, lowering her voice to a whisper. "We don't have a choice, do we?"

Ana drew a deep breath and then exhaled loudly. "I thought this is land of liberty and freedom."

"It is," Rebecca said. "We can choose to walk away—and lose our jobs. But that would be a terrible choice for your family."

As Rebecca said the words, she half-believed them. It was true that ever since Ana's father and brother had been arrested at the strike site, they'd been forbidden to return to work at the coat factory. The family truly did need some emergency income. At the same time, Rebecca had to admit she was working hard on her own behalf, trying to hang on to a golden opportunity.

"And so," Rebecca pressed on, despite her reservations, "this is why we're going to do just as Mr. Hammerstein asked."

"What if he is flimflam man?" Ana asked. "What

if we do this spying and we never get paid for *real* job with Flora? Michael has not been paid yet."

"True, but he hasn't even worked there a week," Rebecca replied. "I'm sure Mr. Hammerstein pays his employees. Why would anyone stay and work for him if he didn't?"

Ana nodded. "Flora seems happy ..."

"Exactly," Rebecca added as they neared their stop. "Besides, Ollie offered to pay for the milk delivery, so we'll earn that money, too. Anything I earn will go to your family. We need to give it a chance."

"All right," Ana said. But her voice was soft, and Rebecca knew she was still worried.

At their subway stop, Michael hopped out first. He pointed to a new, colorful poster that showed elephants balanced on their hind legs.

"Power's Dancing Elephants!" he exclaimed. "Maybe someday I see this show."

That, Rebecca realized, *is why it is so hard to run a theater.* The moment you came up with something fresh and exciting—like a rooftop with a Dutch windmill and farm animals—someone else came up with something even more colossal. Like dancing elephants! No wonder Mr. Hammerstein wanted to know what Mr. Ziegfeld was planning next. No wonder all the performers were so envious of one another. At any moment, something—or someone—new and seemingly better might come along.

As Michael went on to list every show he hoped to see one day, Rebecca let his words wash over her as she did her best to tamp down her lingering concerns. Ana was worried. Their costumes needed washing. And she herself wasn't thrilled about doing farmwork, or about being forced into working as a spy.

But she was going to visit Olivia Berry tomorrow, and despite all her concerns, she couldn't wait!

chapter 4
Break a Leg

IN THE MORNING, Rebecca examined her work uniform, which she'd carefully pinned to the clothesline on the fire escape before bed. She breathed a sigh of relief. She'd managed to scrub out the grass stains on the knees of her overalls, and after a night so warm that she'd slept without a blanket or sheet, her costume was actually dry.

As she packed herself a lunch—challah, cheese, and an apple—Mama stood by, folding laundry.

"Mama," Rebecca said, "I'm so excited to go to my new job again today!"

Planting a kiss on Rebecca's forehead, Mama said, "Ana's family is blessed by your willingness to help out. Now, you girls look out for each other, all right?"

"We will, Mama," Rebecca assured her.

...

Whup-whup-whup. The windmill's sails churned out a greeting as the girls reached the rooftop with Michael. They followed him toward the stage, drawn in by the new scene Mr. O'Hara was painting—a garden of flowers below the Eiffel Tower. His clear tenor voice rang out as he worked:

> *"When Irish eyes are smiling,*
> *sure it's like a morn in spring,*
> *In the lilt of Irish laughter,*
> *You can hear the angels sing!*
> *When Irish hearts are happy*
> *all the world seems bright and gay,*
> *but when Irish eyes are smiling*
> *sure they'll steal your heart away."*

When he finished, Rebecca and Ana clapped. "I think Olivia Berry stole *his* heart away,"

Ana whispered, suppressing a giggle.

"I think so, too," Rebecca said as they headed to the barn.

They found Flora milking a brown cow, who looked back at them with soulful eyes.

"Good morning, girls!" Flora said. She pulled the brimming bucket from under the cow, pushed the wooden stool out of her way with her boot, and carried the bucket to the counter. "Let me just get the milk into the icebox, and then I'll be right with you."

Something sparkled on Flora's ring finger. Rebecca hadn't noticed it the day before. "Your ring is beautiful," she said.

"You are engaged, yes?" Ana asked.

Flora turned to face the girls. Beaming, she twirled the ring on her finger and pressed her palms together, her fingertips touching her red lips.

"Congratulations! Who is he?" Rebecca asked.

Dust specks floated in the barn light. Flora closed

her eyes briefly, smiling to herself, then looked at the girls. "It's Frank, the doorman over at the New Amsterdam. You'll meet him today. He says he sees plenty of beautiful women come and go through the doors, but he's never seen a woman more beautiful—" She stopped and blushed.

Ana finished her sentence. "More beautiful than you."

Flora giggled. "Well, that's what he said."

"When's the wedding?" Rebecca asked.

"As soon as possible! I'd tie the knot today, but Frank says to be patient. He needs to get a day or two off work first." Flora filled a pitcher with milk, tilting the bucket expertly so the pitcher didn't over-flow. "Speaking of work, I'll put Daisy and Dahlia out, and you can get busy on their stalls."

Rebecca scrunched her nose at the smelly cow mess she and Ana would have to clean up. *Maybe it will make the morning go faster,* she thought. *Lunchtime can't come soon enough.*

...

When the sun was straight overhead, Flora rang a small bell outside the barn door. "Lunch break, girls."

"Finally!" Rebecca exclaimed. She tossed a weed into the pile she and Ana had created and hopped to her feet. The knees of her overalls were stained green and brown. Her hands and fingernails were caked with dirt. "I hate to show up at the New Amsterdam like this," she muttered under her breath.

"You don't need to fuss," Flora said, overhearing her. "Olivia Berry thinks she's something special, but those Ziegfeld Girls come and go. You wait and see. Now go wash up inside and get your lunch."

At the little table by the farmhouse window, Rebecca and Ana gobbled down their food and then asked Flora for Ollie's milk.

Flora removed a glass from the icebox and handed it to Rebecca. Then she pulled an envelope from her apron pocket. A faint scent of flowery perfume rose from the note. "Take this, too," she said. "Give it to that handsome doorman, my fiancé. I'm hoping it will help step up our wedding plans." She eyed the full glass of milk in Rebecca's hand. "You'd better take the elevator."

As she and Ana stepped into the elevator, the operator gave them a sideways look. "Down, please," Rebecca said, as if she belonged. "Lobby level."

The operator nodded. "Yes, miss." Rebecca managed not to spill a drop of milk as they crossed the street to the New Amsterdam Theater. On the marquee, flashing lights advertised the new star, Olivia Berry. Billboards highlighted the Ziegfeld Follies' new shows and acts.

"You must be Miss Berry's little sister!" exclaimed the doorman. He had a handlebar mustache and wore a cranberry-colored jacket, pants, and matching cap. "She said you'd be by. You're her spittin' image! Think you'll grow up to be as famous?"

"Well, I'm not really—" Rebecca began.

"Oh, come now, everyone wants to be onstage,"
the doorman went on. "I'm an actor, too, waiting for
that big role to turn up." He swept off his cap, performed a brief tap dance, then took a bow and set the
cap back on his head. "Someday my name will be on
a marquee just like the one above us: Frank Teller,
Song and Dance Man."

"You're Flora's fiancé!" Ana exclaimed.

He nodded. "You can call me Frank."

"I'm Ana. I like theater, but just for watching."

"And I'm Beckie," Rebecca said. "I *love* the stage!
I love acting, especially when I can make people
laugh. I believe it's what I'm meant to do."

"That's the spirit," Frank said.

Rebecca grinned until Ana nudged her, nodding
at her pocket.

"Oh! I almost forgot!" Rebecca said. She reached
into her overalls pocket and pulled out the scented
envelope that bore Frank's name.

He took the envelope and said, "You know, in

addition to acting, I do a bit of magic. Watch carefully." He lifted the plain white envelope toward his nose and inhaled deeply. "This letter was written by someone nearby. I believe it came from ..." He closed his eyes, pushed a forefinger to his temple, as if concentrating very hard, and opened his eyes again. "It's from the Dutch maid, Flora, isn't it?"

Ana laughed. "You already knew is from her!"

Frank smiled. "I had a feeling." He opened the door wide for them to enter and gave them directions to Ollie's dressing room.

Glass of milk in hand, Rebecca led the way. Even if she couldn't be onstage, she told herself, she would play the role of "little sister" to Miss Olivia Berry to the best of her ability. They walked down a hallway decorated with ornate paintings, mirrors, and light fixtures. Rebecca squinted at the brass nameplate on each door they passed. On the very last door, below a shiny star, she read: "OLIVIA BERRY."

The door was open just a crack, and a strange

voice floated from the room. Stepping closer, Rebecca could make out what it was saying: "Pretty baby! Aw, pretty baby!"

Ollie probably has lots of visitors who say that, Rebecca thought.

She tapped hesitantly on the door frame. "I'm sorry to interrupt . . ." she said. "We're here with your milk."

"Come in!" said Ollie. A smile spread across her face as she greeted Rebecca and Ana in her dressing gown. "Sis!"

Her auburn hair was tied in rag curlers, and she wore no makeup. She was still awfully pretty, Rebecca thought, but in a more common way than when she'd visited the rooftop farm yesterday.

"Hello, Miss Berry," Rebecca said.

"Please, from now on, you must call me Ollie. We're supposed to be sisters, remember?" Ollie waved the girls inside. "Go ahead and set the milk on my dressing table."

Rebecca and Ana stepped into the room, where a vase full of roses sat on a small round table. A rotating metal fan cooled the perfume-scented air. Tapestries and mirrors covered every inch of the walls. A corner rack boasted hanger after hanger of silks and feathers, ruffles and furs. Behind a pink velvet chaise, lacy slips and underclothes were draped over the top of a flowered dressing screen. Every inch of the room oozed *luxury.* But where was Ollie's visitor?

"Pretty baby!" The voice came again, and Rebecca whirled around to look. Perched inside a cage in one corner of the room was a large white bird with long feathers at the crown of its head.

"Oh!" Rebecca exclaimed. Even Ollie's pets were astounding! "How beautiful! I've never seen a bird like that!"

Ollie opened the cage door, and let the bird climb up her arm and onto her shoulder. "Meet my new best friend, Sweetie. He's a cockatoo.

He was a gift from my boyfriend."

"Pretty baby!" Sweetie squawked again and again, bobbing his head up and down.

Sweetie tipped his head and watched curiously as Ollie sat down at the dressing table, removed her rag curlers, and began to apply her makeup. The bright bulbs surrounding the mirror illuminated everything on the table—jars of creams and powders, tiny pots of lip paint, compacts of rouge, and glistening perfume bottles.

A large glass bowl showcasing unusual candies caught Rebecca's eye, and she bent to get a closer look. They were not candies! The bowl was brimming with rings, earrings, brooches, and necklaces of jade, pearls, rubies, sapphires, and diamonds, all set in gold and silver.

"Are they real?" Rebecca asked, full of wonder.

"No, but they sparkle just as much!" Ollie said, laughing lightly. "My boyfriend isn't the only one who gives me lovely gifts. You wouldn't believe what gets left here for me by people I don't know and will never meet."

"Fans?" Rebecca asked. "Like Mr. O'Hara?"

"He's just one among many." Ollie shrugged. "Can you believe it? So many hopeful suitors. They buy gifts, but they can't buy love. Try as they might, I only have eyes for one." She nodded toward a frame on the dressing table. It held a photo of an older man in a light suit coat, his oiled-back hair exposing a high forehead. "You're looking at the man who owns this theater. He started the Follies. Before I met Ziggy, I'd been on the cover of many magazines, but he gave me my first real break here on the stage. I've always wanted to act."

"Oh, me too!" Rebecca said, entranced.

"Who doesn't?" Ollie said.

"I do not," Ana said. "Many people have other dreams."

Ollie glanced back at Ana in the mirror. "Remind me, it's Beckie and . . . ?"

"Ana," she answered.

"Well, no matter what you dream of," Ollie said, turning to face Ana directly, "you will need to get rid of that accent. You can, you know, if you work at it. Lots of girls do. If you're ambitious and want to get anywhere, you need to distance yourself from your humble origins."

Ana frowned. "I am not ashamed being from Russia—" she began, but Ollie had already turned away and picked up her milk. She tipped the glass back in one long drink and then stood up.

"Hey, little dollies," she said. "Let me get Sweetie settled back in his cage, and I'll give you a tour. You might even catch a glimpse of our rehearsal for next week's big show. Would you like that?"

"More than anything!" Rebecca answered.

"Then let's go." Ollie gently lifted Sweetie from her shoulder, set him on his perch, and closed the cage door. "I'm sure Flora wants you back as soon as possible."

...

The girls hurried behind Ollie as she pushed through a side door into the theater and motioned Rebecca and Ana to take seats in the front row.

Rebecca couldn't believe her eyes. The theater was a fairyland, lushly painted, with gilded box seats above and a grand stage below.

And onstage! A horse reared up as its handsome rider twirled a rope above his head. Rebecca immediately recognized the man as the famous cowboy star, Will Rogers. He smiled widely as the horse dropped its front hooves to the stage and turned in dizzying circles. Then he wheeled the horse to a sudden stop, leaped off, and began spinning his rope down low, jumping in and out of the loop. A spotlight followed the star as he nonchalantly strolled about the stage, never letting the lasso stop. "Well, what shall I talk about?" he began. "I ain't got anything funny to say. All I know is what I read in the papers."

"Now he'll tell a few jokes about what's in the news," Ollie said. She squeezed Rebecca's hand. "My part's next, so I can't stay." She slipped out of her seat and disappeared toward the stage.

"And so on . . ." Will Rogers called out after a few minutes, signaling the end of his run-through. "I don't wanna wear out my jokes."

As he walked offstage, Ana turned to Rebecca. "We should go now," she whispered. "Flora will be not happy if—"

"Just a few more minutes," Rebecca insisted. "We can't leave before Ollie performs!"

Ana gave Rebecca a pleading look, but sat back in her seat.

A tune floated up from the orchestra pit, just in front of the stage. The conductor's baton danced up and down. Stage lights dimmed, and a single beam focused on Ollie, seated midair on an ornate swing as it slowly descended toward the stage. Even in her dressing gown, she looked like a star.

At the same moment, Will Rogers took a seat
a couple of rows behind Rebecca and Ana and
stretched his fancy-stitched cowboy boots out in
front of him. The smell of leather floated in the air.
Rebecca turned and grinned at him.

"A shopgirl," he muttered loudly enough for
Rebecca to hear. "Ziegfeld insisted on her. With all
the fanfare, let's hope she can do more than look
pretty on that swing."

"That's rude," Rebecca whispered back. She
hoped she hadn't been rude herself in saying so, but
how could she not defend her new friend? And what
was wrong with being a shopgirl? Rebecca herself
had worked hard at Papa's shop many times.

Rebecca's train of thought stopped short the
moment Ollie started to sing. Olivia Berry's voice
was as lovely and sweet as her face. Even Will Rogers
stayed silent.

As Ollie finished her song, the spotlight dimmed,
and the closing notes of the orchestra drifted upward.

Ollie stepped lightly off the swing and curtsied with a nod of her curls. Then she smiled at Rebecca, brought her fingers to her lips, and blew her a kiss.

Rebecca flushed. How special she felt! It really *was* like she was Ollie's little sister!

The house lights went up, breaking the mood, and when a man with slicked-back hair stepped into the theater through a side door, Ollie's gaze pivoted to him. With a good-bye wave to Rebecca and Ana, she skipped down the stage stairs and left, her hand resting lightly on the arm of the man's pale linen suit.

It was the man in the photo, Rebecca realized—Mr. Ziegfeld, the owner of the New Amsterdam Theater and producer of the Ziegfeld Follies.

"We must go now," Ana whispered. "Is late."

Together, the girls skirted the stage toward the exit door, passing two dancers who lingered onstage.

"When I tell her 'break a leg' for luck," one said, "I really mean it! I'd love to see her break a leg—or worse," she snickered.

Shocked, Rebecca turned and met the icy glare of a blonde woman with a button nose and heavily penciled eyebrows.

"Shhh! That one's her little sister!" the other dancer hissed as Rebecca and Ana passed.

Rebecca remembered Ollie's comment in the barn about not having found many friends among the other Ziegfeld Girls. Now there was no doubt why. The air here was so thick with jealousy that you could practically cut it with a knife.

chapter 5
Drastic Action

WHEN REBECCA AND Ana stepped outside the theater, Frank tipped his cranberry-colored hat. "Have a good day, ladies! Say hello to Flora for me."

"We will!" Ana said.

Hand in hand, the girls watched for an opening in traffic, hurried across the street, and raced up the stairs to the rooftop.

Flora was waiting for them inside the barn. "You girls are fifteen minutes late!"

"We are sorry, Flora!" Ana said.

"We'll make up for it tomorrow," Rebecca said.

"Yes, you *will* make up for it tomorrow. In the morning, you'll go to Central Park. We've done business with the goat keeper there before. You will buy a goat from him and bring it here."

"A goat?" Ana repeated.

Flora nodded. "That's what I said. Sadly, we lost a goat last week, and we need to replace it."

"What happened to the goat?" Rebecca asked.

Flora glanced at Ana and paused, as if reluctant to answer. "Goats—they eat just about anything. And some of the things they get into aren't good for them." Then she swiftly changed the subject to an explanation of how, exactly, to buy a goat.

"All right," Rebecca said when Flora had finished. "But what if we're late delivering milk to Miss Berry?"

"Will you please stop fussing about Ollie?" Flora rolled her eyes skyward. "Does the whole of New York City have to cater to her? I'll see to it that her milk gets delivered tomorrow." After a pause, she went on. "Mr. O'Hara has mentioned a friend backstage at the New Amsterdam who can let him in. I'll ask him to take it over on his lunch break. He'll be walking on clouds all day."

With a nod, Rebecca held her tongue. At least, she thought, she and Ana had gathered enough information to appease Mr. Hammerstein when they reported to him at the end of the day.

Mr. Hammerstein waved the girls into his office with an impatient flick of his hand. "Girls!" he growled. "Have you been keeping your eyes and ears open?"

Spying? Rebecca wanted to say, but didn't. "Yes, sir," she said.

Mr. Hammerstein leaned forward. "Don't keep me in suspense a moment longer."

"Well, Olivia Berry is the star of the show . . ." Rebecca hesitated. Saying Ollie's name out loud to Mr. Hammerstein was an uncomfortable reminder of the position she was in. How could she keep Mr. Hammerstein happy and avoid betraying her new friend?

"Olivia Berry!" Mr. Hammerstein barked. "Tell

me something I don't know. She'll be just like every other pretty face: on the marquee for a moment, then gone forever."

Was it true? Rebecca wondered. *Could someone like Ollie be so easily replaced or outdone?* Rebecca couldn't help feeling indignant on Ollie's behalf.

"But she's not just another pretty face," Rebecca protested. "She sings beautifully, too."

"So do canaries," Mr. Hammerstein said. "So what?"

"She sits on a swing that lowers from the ceiling," Rebecca added before she could stop herself. "It's really something."

Mr. Hammerstein seemed unimpressed. "A swing. Already bringing in the novelties to pump up the act. Mark my words, that girl won't last."

Rebecca's cheeks grew hot. If Mr. Ziegfeld, the owner of the New Amsterdam, recognized how special Ollie was, why couldn't Mr. Hammerstein? Forgetting all about her intention to hold her tongue, she leaped to Ollie's defense. "Mr. Ziegfeld gave her a very special gift," Rebecca blurted. "An exotic tropical bird. He seems to think that she is very important."

"A bird, you say?" Mr. Hammerstein asked, stroking his chin. Then he shrugged. "Nothing but romance. Tell me something I can use."

"She—" Rebecca began.

"Will Rogers is in show," Ana interjected. "He rode horse right onstage! He did tricks with rope."

"Did he now?" Mr. Hammerstein scowled. "You know, that fella got his start in my theater years ago. Now he bounces around theaters like a badminton birdie! Draws crowds wherever he performs."

The room fell silent as Mr. Hammerstein lit his cigar. "Swings, horses, Will Rogers. Could be serious competition," he said finally. He took a deep puff from the cigar, then pursed his lips. "This may call for drastic action."

Rebecca swallowed hard and shared a look of concern with Ana. What could Mr. Hammerstein mean by "drastic action?" Did he mean he was going to pump up his own acts? Or—she swallowed again—would he try to cause problems for the New Amsterdam Theater somehow? And would that cause problems for Ollie? Was he that much of a flimflam man? Rebecca left Mr. Hammerstein's office with Ana, wishing with all her heart she could take back every word she'd just said.

The next morning, as planned, the girls waited outside the theater until a truck with "THE VICTORY THEATER" painted in swirling letters on its side pulled up alongside them. "Hop in," the driver said. "Heard you need a ride to Central Park."

"That's right," Rebecca answered. With Flora's money for the goat tucked in her pocket, she felt important—and nervous. Mr. Hammerstein's comment about "drastic action" was still fresh in her mind. While she wasn't sure what he'd meant, she did know that he put his theater's success above everything. Even if he had no intention of causing trouble for his archrival, he wouldn't hesitate a second to fire her and Ana if they didn't perform their jobs properly.

At the south end of the park, the driver parked. "I'll wait here," he said, and doffed his cap as they climbed out. "Don't take all day."

"We will hurry," Ana said.

Rebecca hooked her arm with Ana's and scanned the greenery ahead. "We can't afford to get lost," she said. She knew the park was huge—as big as some small towns. It had both a main zoo and a children's zoo. It also had bridges, countless fountains and sculptures, ponds, and even a lake. Carriage drivers offered rides to customers, and horse owners rode along the park's many paths.

As the girls neared the goat pen, a steady stream of little carts carrying groups of squealing children passed them by. The carts were pulled by goats and looked like miniature carriages—with upholstered seats, oil lamps, and drivers in black caps and uniforms—but the drivers were boys not much older than Rebecca. As soon as each cart returned and one set of children hopped out, another set hopped in.

A crowd was gathering at the goat pen as the girls reached it. Three black-and-white baby goats inside the pen were putting on quite a show, leaping, hopping, twisting, and turning. A white-haired man and a big dog with a mottled coat stood nearby, keeping an eye on the flock. One of the baby goats jumped onto the dog's broad back. A second goat followed, and then a third—until, too crowded, they all tumbled off and bounded around the pen again. When the man reached down to pick up an overturned bucket, a baby goat leaped through the air and landed on his back. It straddled the man's head, its front and back feet on his shoulders, as he straightened. Taking the goat by its legs, the man gently set it to the ground. The crowd clapped enthusiastically, and the man took a bow.

"The world's a stage!" Rebecca said to Ana. "Even the goats enjoy putting on a show!" As she watched them, an idea began to take shape in her head. "If it were up to me, I'd take all three babies back with us. That would really step up the show at the Victory."

Rebecca eyed Ana, hoping for a sign that her cousin agreed. "It would keep Mr. Hammerstein happy," she pressed on. *And then maybe he won't push us to reveal so much about Ollie and her show.*

"I think Flora does not want—" Ana began. She was interrupted by a small girl in a ruffled white dress who tugged on the leg of her overalls.

"Can my brother and I get a ride next?" asked the girl. She and the boy beside her, in a crisp shirt and creased trousers, looked expectantly from Ana to Rebecca.

"We don't work here," Rebecca replied.

"You look like you do," the boy said.

Ana folded her arms across her chest. "Not everybody can play and spend money on goat rides," she muttered as the children moved on. "Some of us must work."

"True," Rebecca whispered, suddenly feeling sorry that Ana felt so burdened by her responsibilities. "Those kids might have money to buy a ride, but I bet we're the only ones with money in hand to buy a whole goat! Why don't we have a little fun with this? Let's act like we're rich!"

Ana gave her cousin a dubious look, but Rebecca strode ahead to the pen, hand on her hip and one forefinger pressed to her lips, as if she were considering a big decision.

"Ana, *dah-ling*," Rebecca said, feigning her best British accent, "we *must* purchase only the best goat available. It must be worthy of an audience, for we represent the theater. Don't you agree?"

She cast a sideways glance at Ana, hoping her cousin would begin to play along. But Ana stayed silent. Rebecca lifted her chin and went on. "As our dear friend, Mr. Hammerstein, likes to say, we must treat every day as if it is opening night. And that goes for our goats!"

A white billy goat with pale eyes pressed his front hooves to the top of the fence and stretched his horns and head toward the girls. "I daresay he's asking to be scratched," Rebecca said, pointing, in hopes Ana would take the cue.

"I . . . I daresay he is!" Ana said at last. She reached over the fence and scratched between the goat's wide-set eyes, which he closed in bliss. A foul, oily smell rose from his coat.

"He bothers my nose," Ana declared, grimacing.

Rebecca leaned toward the goat and sniffed. "Sorry, old chum. You won't do."

The elderly man minding the goats rose from a wooden bench in the enclosure. The three baby goats trotted to greet him and then went back to their antics. Almost as soon as they started, a new audience gathered to laugh and clap.

"Those babies draw the best audience," Rebecca

whispered to Ana. "We really should get those. Flora will understand."

"Is big risk," Ana said under her breath. "Maybe we lose jobs. Maybe Michael loses his."

"Ana, trust me," Rebecca said. "I have an instinct about what audiences like. This will keep Mr. Hammerstein on our side." She pressed ahead, extending her hand in the air. "Sir? How much for all three of the little ones?"

"How much you want to pay?" he answered.

Rebecca knew the man was inviting her to bargain. She squared her shoulders and flashed a confident smile. "Three baby goats for the price of one full-grown," she offered.

The man considered Rebecca's proposal for a mere second. "You have a deal," he said, clapping his hands together. Then he gave them his going price for a goat.

"Is too high," Ana said. She turned to Rebecca as if she'd been insulted. She pointed to two goats with extra wide bellies. "You have more babies soon, I think."

The man nodded. When he named a slightly lower price, Rebecca resisted the urge to jump at it. She knew there could still be wiggle room in the price. She shrugged, linked arms with Ana, and strolled away.

"Wait," the man called. "It's almost the end of the season. I don't need to keep feeding extra little ones all winter. With more babies coming, we will be short on room. I don't know why, but today, I'll give you my rock-bottom price."

Smiling at each other, the girls turned back. Rebecca counted out Flora's money, and the girls struggled out of the park to the street with the baby goats twisting and tugging on their ropes. The goats bleated and beeped, making such funny sounds that Rebecca's sides hurt from laughing. "I hope Flora agrees that these goats will be crowd-pleasers!" she said when she caught her breath.

"I hope, too," Ana said.

They found the theater truck parked exactly where they'd left it. Rebecca knocked on the passenger window, and the driver's eyes sprang open. Spotting the three goats, he shook his head. "In back with the lot of you," he said.

The girls lifted the little goats one by one into the back of the truck, then clambered in themselves, crouching under a canopy. As the truck pulled away, one of the goats started bleating, which set the other two off. Ana put her fingers in her ears. When one goat climbed up on Ana's back and settled on her shoulders like a shawl, Rebecca started giggling and couldn't stop. Riding in a truck was a rare opportunity, but riding with baby goats? That was a once-in-a-lifetime experience! When school started again and she was asked to write about her summer, she doubted her teacher would even believe this story.

"What if Flora is very mad?" Ana shouted over the rumble of the truck and the baby goats' complaints.

Rebecca bit her lip. "She won't be. The goats will be a hit," she insisted, even as a tiny voice inside her was saying something different. *What if I was wrong?*

It was early afternoon by the time the girls returned to the Victory. They headed straight for the elevator.

When the doors opened, the operator looked at them, and then at the animals. "We are delivering them to the top," Rebecca said, as if it were the most natural thing in the world to step into an elevator with three baby goats.

"Very well," the man replied. "Step in." He slid the doors shut, pulled a lever, and set the elevator in motion.

"It's very warm in here today," Ana said, fanning herself.

"Yes, but it gets even hotter when customers arrive," the man said. "It is Mr. Hammerstein's *best* trick. On summer nights, people go to the roof to cool off. But some nights they complain that it's not

cool enough. He first tried blowing fans over blocks
of ice in the basement and pumping cool air up to
the rooftop. Still, customers complained of the heat.
So he got a new idea. Make the elevator hotter! Now
customers step out and say, 'Oh, it's much better
on top!' Clever, no?"

Rebecca smiled politely. But it didn't sound quite
right to her.

As the elevator ascended, Rebecca wondered what
other tricks Mr. Hammerstein had up his sleeve. She
knew that bargaining for the goats required a bit of
bluffing. But haggling over a price was a two-sided
game, a dance that both the seller and the buyer
stepped into, knowing they would each gain from
a sale. And there was a difference between a trick
that entertains, like Michael's coin tricks, and a trick
that takes advantage of others. There was something
dishonest about Mr. Hammerstein's elevator scheme,
Rebecca thought, but she couldn't decide if that made
him a thief. At the very least, she decided, he *was* a

flimflam man. He dazzled people into giving him
their money.

As the elevator doors opened, Rebecca willed
her concerns away. The girls thanked the operator
and hurried out after the goats. Straining at the end
of their ropes, all three goats rose up on their hind
legs, seeming to plead, "Look at me! Look at me!"
They paddled their front hooves in the air as if they
couldn't *wait* to start entertaining customers.

"Three goats?!" Flora said as soon as she saw
the girls with their brood. She stood outside the
barn, hands on her hips, watching the baby goats lap
water from a bucket. "I asked you to buy *one*. How
many is that? Do either of you know how to count?"

Ana held up one finger.

"Beckie" Flora said, "why do I get the feeling this
was your idea? You know your position here hangs by
a thread, especially if you can't follow instructions."

Rebecca opened her mouth to speak, but Ana
chimed in instead.

"We will take them back," Ana said, her head bowed. "I am sorry. Rebecca thought goats would be good for show."

"There it is," Flora said. "At least I know who to blame. Beckie, do you think you're becoming high and mighty like Miss Olivia Berry? You can just do whatever you please?"

Rebecca's stomach twisted. She'd been overly confident. What if she and Ana were dismissed because she didn't do as she was asked? She met Flora's gaze. "It *was* all my idea. I thought they would make customers laugh. We can take them back, I'm sure, and trade them for one goat. My heart got ahead of me, I guess."

Flora's expression softened, and she squared her shoulders. "Well, I suppose our hearts *do* get ahead of our minds sometimes," she said after a moment. A coy smile bloomed on her face, and Rebecca guessed Flora was thinking about Frank. "And they are quite cute. Let's get them over to the goat pen.

How about we give it a day? We'll see how things go, and decide tomorrow."

The girls exchanged glances and nodded.

Once untied in the pen, the baby goats danced, leaped, and greeted the older goats. Soon one baby was standing on the back of a much larger, shaggy black goat, who didn't seem to mind. Another ran under the legs of a gray-and-white goat. And the third leaped into a trough as Ana filled it with grain.

A brash laugh came from outside the pen. With a glance, Rebecca knew who it was. Standing beside Flora, Mr. Hammerstein watched appreciatively as the baby goats leaped, hopped, and pranced.

"A splendid addition!" he boomed. "Folks will lap it up!"

"I'm delighted you approve!" Flora said.

Rebecca let out a sigh. *Our jobs are safe,* she thought. *At least for the moment.*

chapter 6

Three Times
the Trouble

ON TUESDAY MORNING, the moment
Rebecca, Ana, and Michael reached the top of the
staircase and opened the door to the Victory rooftop,
Mr. O'Hara charged toward them, waving his arms
and shaking his head of red curls.

"Michael! Flora's fit to be tied! The goats have run
amok! We need to fix the whole shebang before we
can get to painting."

"Oh no!" Rebecca took off running toward the
massive flowerpots at the edge of the rooftop. All
three baby goats were munching the flowers in one
of the pots. "Ana, come help!"

Rebecca grabbed one goat and set it down. Then
she snatched up another and held it in her arms. It
bleated and squealed in complaint. "Ana, hang on to

that one. If we walk two of them back to their pen,
I bet the third one will follow."

Her plan worked, but when Rebecca inspected the
pen, she saw that the baby goats had pushed through
small openings at the bottom of the fencing. If they
were returned to the pen with the bigger goats, they'd
be back out again in no time. Michael and Mr. O'Hara
would need to secure the goat pen before the goats
could be put back in it.

"Ana, follow me," Rebecca said. The goat in her
arms licked her cheek as she and Ana walked into the
barn, shutting the door behind their bleating compan-
ions. They found Flora in the first stall, milking a cow.

"Shouldn't have let them stay," Flora said, not
even looking up. "But Mr. Hammerstein approved,
so I can hardly send them back now. You'll have to
keep an eye on them until we get the pen fixed."

"Sorry for the trouble," Rebecca said, as she set
down a wiggling goat. With the barn door closed,
the goats bounded around the space until the girls

secured collars around their necks.

"It was bound to happen," Flora said with a glance. "The pen needed some work anyway. Any critter with half a brain will keep looking until it finds the holes. Now that we know where the weak spots are, we can fix them."

Rebecca thought spying was a little like that. At least, that's how it would be if Mr. Hammerstein used the information he gathered from their spying scheme only to fix any weak spots at his own theater. She hoped against hope he wasn't using it for something worse.

The girls spent the morning restoring order as the goats strained on their ropes, threatening to make new messes. During the night, the little goats had been in the vegetable and flower gardens and left little muddy tracks across the stage floor. Just before lunch—and just when they thought they'd finished everything—Ana showed Rebecca two theater seats that had been thoroughly chewed. Rebecca let out a gasp so loud that Michael and Mr. O'Hara came running.

"This is bad," Rebecca said.

"We are in big trouble," Ana said. "We cannot pay! Will we go to jail?"

Mr. O'Hara bent over one seat to inspect the damage. As he tried to poke the stuffing back into the cushion, his metal flask slipped out of his pocket onto the floor, dislodging its cork. A clear liquid dribbled from the flask onto the floor.

Just then, one of the goats managed to wriggle out of his rope. In a flash, he dashed to the puddle and began to lick it up.

"Shoo! Away with ye!" Mr. O'Hara shouted, snatching up the flask as Rebecca tugged the goat back from the spill. Mr. O'Hara recorked the flask, slipped it back in his coat pocket, and gave the goat a little scratch between the ears. "Sure'n you'd be sorry if you drank that, ye silly beast!"

Remembering what Flora had said about

goats—they would eat anything, even if it wasn't good for them—Rebecca was grateful Mr. O'Hara had shooed the little animal away. She was even more grateful when, after a few more attempts to poke the stuffing back in the chairs, Mr. O'Hara straightened up, brushed his hands, and announced that he and Michael could simply replace the chair cushions.

"There are more cushions just like these in the basement near the paint cabinets," he said. "Michael and I can put 'em in before Mr. Hammerstein ever notices."

Ana heaved a huge sigh. "Thank you, Mr. O'Hara!"

"Yes, thank you!" Rebecca added, feeling suddenly sheepish that she and Ana had laughed so hard about his feelings for Ollie. Like a knight, he'd just saved them from dragons—or at least the wrath of Flora and Mr. Hammerstein.

• • •

The girls gobbled lunch to make up for lost time. Snatching up the glass Flora had set aside for Ollie, Rebecca accidentally let milk slosh over the side. "Oops!" she said. When she took a sip to make the glass less full and easier to carry, her mouth puckered. "Flora!" she called out. "Something's wrong with the milk!"

Flora hurried down the ladder from the hayloft. "Here, let me check," she said, raising the glass to her lips and taking a sip. "Oh, my! That batch is from yesterday. Must be going bad fast in this heat." She dumped the milk down the sink. After filling a new glass with fresh milk and handing it to Rebecca, Flora turned to the counter and handed Rebecca another envelope. This one was pink, with fancy-cut paper edges. "Please give this to Frank," she said.

"Another love note?" Ana asked with a smile.

Flora beamed, lifting her hands in mock protest. As she did so, sunlight caught the diamond in her ring, sending sparkles of light dancing around the barn.

...

"For you," Ana said, handing the letter to Frank.

"Another note?" His right eyebrow shot up, as if he couldn't be more surprised. How Rebecca wished she could do that with her eyebrow!

Frank jammed the letter in his pocket with scarcely a glance, reached for the door and opened it wide. "Ladies!" he said, tipping his hat.

"I love this job," Rebecca whispered as she and Ana stepped into the shadowy building. Picturing the whole theater filled to the brim with eager patrons in the evening, she felt a tiny thrill at the thought that none of them would see what she was seeing right this moment—the inner workings of the theater world.

They arrived at Ollie's dressing room only to find it empty, except for Sweetie, who called to them from his cage. "Pretty baby!" He cocked his head and did an impatient little dance on his perch.

"Sorry, Sweetie," Rebecca said. "No time to talk now." She set the milk on Ollie's table and looked around. "Ana, we're a little late. I bet Ollie's already started rehearsal. Let's see if we can catch her act!"

As they made their way to the theater, Rebecca said, "Isn't Sweetie just the most adorable thing?"

"Yes," Ana agreed. "But Olivia Berry does not need anyone else to tell her she is pretty."

"Well, she is," Rebecca said matter-of-factly.

"Pretty can be problem." Ana's expression grew serious. "My teacher talked about Greek myths. What is name of handsome young man who loved looking in the pool of water?"

"Narcissus," Rebecca said. She'd heard of him, too.

Ana nodded. "He fell in love with the image of himself. All day, he look at his face in the water. Nothing else!"

"Well, Ollie's not like that," Rebecca said. "She's not just pretty. She has real talent. And she genuinely loves her work. I can tell."

The girls fell silent as they entered the hushed theater. They took seats in the back of the theater just as Will Rogers was telling his last few jokes, then waited in the semidarkness as performers scurried about, a director shouted instructions, and the orchestra tuned their instruments. After what seemed like forever, Ollie began her descent by swing to the center of the stage. This time the spotlight was tinted blue, and Ollie wore translucent indigo wings. The effect was stunning! Rebecca loved to see how each run-through allowed the director to make the show its very best.

Treat each day like opening night. Rebecca was sure that everyone here was living by that motto.

From where they sat, Rebecca could see some movement from the wing at stage right. Squinting, she spotted the two dancers who had grumbled about Ollie the other day watching from behind the curtains, whispering to each other. A man slipped into the shadows behind them, but Rebecca couldn't make out who he was. A stagehand? Mr. Ziegfeld? It took so many people to put on a show.

Ollie's voice rose clear and strong, and Rebecca's heart swelled to know that the beautiful, talented Miss Olivia Berry was her friend. Then, as the swing hovered ten or fifteen feet above the stage, Rebecca heard a twang, like a broken guitar string—followed by Ollie's scream.

chapter 7

The Green-Eyed Monster

THE ORCHESTRA STOPPED playing. Ollie dangled from the broken swing, with one hand clinging to the remaining cable.

The director flew onto the stage toward Ollie. From the opposite direction came another man, who raced under the swing and, just as Ollie lost her grip on the cable, managed to snag her by the waist. Though the move slowed her fall, Ollie's head flopped backward and hit the stage floor— hard. The man gently lowered her the rest of the way onto the floor and dropped to his knees beside her. "Thank the stars above I was here for you," he said. "Oh dear! I saw it all. Say something, me fair rose."

The lilting Irish accent was unmistakable. "It's

Mr. O'Hara!" Rebecca exclaimed. She turned to Ana. "Flora said he had a friend backstage. I bet he comes to watch Ollie perform!"

"Is good thing he was there!" Ana said.

But in the next moment, the director had elbowed Mr. O'Hara aside and was scooping Ollie up in his arms. "Step back!" he ordered. "Let's get her to the dressing room. She needs a doctor."

Her heart in her throat, Rebecca watched as the director and Mr. O'Hara carried Ollie offstage, just past the spot where the two Ziegfeld Girls had been standing just before Ollie's act. But the women were already gone. To Rebecca, something about their swift disappearance was troubling.

"Ana, wait here." Rebecca jumped up. She wanted a closer look at Ollie's swing before anyone had a chance to fix or remove it. It had worked perfectly well a few days earlier, she thought. Why had it failed so suddenly? Head high, Rebecca walked to the front of the stage, climbed a short flight of stairs, and strode to the spot where Ollie had fallen. The swing's wooden seat hung like a broken arm. The cable dangled down to Rebecca's shoulder height.

Rebecca took hold of the damaged cable and examined it closely. If it had snapped solely from Ollie's weight, she reasoned, the individual wires that made up the cable would look uneven and frayed. Instead, only a few strands of wire were frayed. All the other cable wires looked neatly cut—as though they had been snipped clean through.

Oh! Rebecca stifled a gasp. This was no accident—someone had deliberately cut the cable! A few strands had been left in place—to break once Ollie got on the swing, at the worst possible moment. Her stomach turned at the thought.

"Oi, missy!" came a voice. "Shouldn't ye be getting back where ye belong?" Glancing up, Rebecca met Mr. O'Hara's gaze. Another man in paint-speckled trousers stood behind him.

"Looks like neither one of us can resist a

performance by Miss Berry," Mr. O'Hara said jovially, though his forehead was creased with concern. "My friend here, Mr. Petrov, is the set painter at the New Amsterdam." The other man nodded in greeting. "Pete lets me in the stage door at lunch to watch the rehearsals. I've seen nearly every practice. Never such a blunder as this!" He shook his head, and a note of anger colored his voice. "Were I Mr. Ziegfeld, I'd have the director fired for it. 'Tis terrible."

Rebecca nodded. The seriousness of Ollie's accident suddenly hit her, and tears sprang to her eyes. "I need to see if Ollie's okay."

"Please send my regards," Mr. O'Hara said, doffing his cap and holding it to his chest as she turned away.

Rebecca hopped off the stage and hurried back to the seats where Ana waited. "We still have a little time before we have to be back at the Victory. Let's go see if Ollie's in her room," Rebecca said. "There's something I need to tell her."

Just as she lifted her hand to knock, the door to Ollie's dressing room opened, releasing the sweet smell of perfume. An imposing man stood in the doorway, hand still on the doorknob, his eyebrows furrowed in concern.

"Now don't go worrying about me, Ziggy," Ollie called out after him. "I'm going to be just fine."

"You must take care of yourself, darling," the man said. "The show's in just a few days."

Then he noticed Rebecca and Ana. "No visitors!" he barked.

"Hello, Mr. Ziegfeld. I want to check on my sister," Rebecca said quickly, realizing that if he took her for just another fan, she might be told to leave before she could speak with Ollie.

"Sister?" he said, looking to Ollie, who forced a smile.

"It's okay, Ziggy. I was expecting them. You can go," Ollie said. "Come in, sis."

The moment Rebecca pulled the door shut

behind her and Ana, Ollie stretched out on her chaise and closed her eyes. With a groan, she reached behind her head, and her eyes flew open again. "I have a bump on the back of my head the size of an egg!" She motioned to Ana. "Can you get me some ice?"

"But where—" Ana began.

"I don't know!" Ollie's voice was irritable. "I'm sure you can figure it out!"

Rebecca spotted a silver bucket and handed it to Ana, who shot her a look of bafflement and hurt at Ollie's tone. *Ollie does sound awfully crabby,* Rebecca thought. But then again, she'd just taken a bad fall with a hit to the back of her head. Rebecca gave her cousin a sympathetic smile. She hoped she could smooth things over with Ana later.

Ollie rubbed her head and moaned softly. "I must get the swelling down before the doctor gets here," she said. "I can't have him ordering bed rest." A rattle came from Sweetie's cage. The cockatoo wove back and forth in front of the metal door, stopping every so often to shake the bars with his beak. "Poor dear desperately wants out. Open his door, will you?"

The moment Rebecca did so, Sweetie flapped to Ollie's lap. He bowed his head, and Ollie stroked his head feathers. "There," Ollie cooed. "Nobody wants to be stuck in a cage, now, do they?"

For a moment, Rebecca wondered if Ollie was talking about herself or the bird. *Maybe both,* she thought. The life of a vaudeville star was harder than it seemed.

Rebecca looked around for more ways to be helpful. The glass of milk she'd brought to the room earlier was still where she'd left it. "Do you want your milk?" she asked.

"Sure," Ollie said, taking the glass. She drank half the milk and set the glass back down. "It's just so strange. I've been on the swing all week with no problem. Why now?"

Sweetie flapped from Ollie's lap to the makeup table. He pecked at his image in the mirror. "Pretty baby!" he cooed. Then he turned to the half-empty glass of milk, dipped his beak and head inside it, and lifted his head to swallow.

"Sweetie, no!" Ollie said, but Sweetie returned to the milk for another drink. When his head appeared stuck, he squawked and pulled back, nearly knocking over the glass. Rebecca grabbed for the glass and steadied it. Sweetie tipped his head back for one last swallow.

"Well, I guess I won't be drinking the rest of that!" Ollie said, half-laughing. Then she winced and leaned back again.

Rebecca drew a breath and told Ollie what she'd discovered about the swing. "I think someone wants to stop you from being onstage," she concluded. "Can you think of who it might be?"

"A green-eyed monster, that's who," Ollie replied, her voice somber. She stroked Sweetie again. "That's another name for envy. And just about all the Ziegfeld Girls are envious of me. Some of those gals have been working toward my spot for years. I come in, a complete newcomer, and get star billing. It's not my fault, but that doesn't mean they like it."

"Ana and I overheard two of them saying mean things about you," Rebecca said. "The blonde one said she'd like to see you 'break a leg—or worse.'"

"That would be Tilly—Tilly Parker," said Ollie. "She's been here the longest. And she talks the loudest, that's for sure."

It seemed to Rebecca that Ollie was acting way too casual about her situation. "If she cut the swing's cable, that's serious," she said, pushing ahead. "I think you need to tell Mr. Ziegfeld what's going on around here."

Ollie's voice turned steely. "I will do no such thing. Ziggy insists we girls never bring our squabbles to him. We need to work things out on our own. Besides, no one wants a scandal."

"But I'm worried about you," Rebecca pleaded. "What if the cable had snapped when you were up near the ceiling?"

Just then, there was a soft knock at the door and Ana stepped back inside. "I found ice," she said quietly.

Rebecca found a towel on the dresser and handed it to Ollie, who took a few chunks of ice from the silver bucket, wrapped them in the towel, and wedged it behind her head. Then, fixing her gaze on Rebecca, she spoke, her voice even and crystal clear. "I am not about to start causing trouble. And neither will you."

Outside the New Amsterdam, before heading back across the street, Rebecca told Frank about Ollie's fall from the swing.

He clapped his hand to his heart, as if the news had stopped it from beating.

"I think someone wanted to hurt her," Rebecca said.

"But who would do such a thing?" Frank said, his eyes watery with concern. "And why? Sure, there's backstabbing and jealousy in show business, but this . . ." He stopped, as if thunderstruck by the news. Then he took Rebecca's hands in his and shook them up and down. "Thank you for letting me know about our dear Miss Berry. I—I'm going to keep an extra lookout for anything suspicious around here."

As the girls approached the curb to cross the street, Frank stepped in front of them and held them back. He walked into traffic, blew a whistle, and held up his arm like a police officer. He stopped a carriage heading one way and a shiny black car heading the other. When the girls safely reached the other side of the street, Rebecca called back, "Thank you, Frank!"

From his side of the street, Frank swept his hat off and bowed.

"Flora is lucky," Ana said. "He is nice."

"Very nice," Rebecca agreed. But she wondered about the way he'd clapped his hand over his heart. He seemed as smitten by Ollie as Mr. O'Hara was—not like a man engaged to be married to someone else.

chapter 8

A Shadow Falls

"IF THESE BABY goats are to stay," Flora said when the girls returned, "they need to be fresh and clean."

As the afternoon heat climbed, Rebecca was grateful to sink her hands into the cool, wet coat of a wiggly goat as it stood in the metal washtub. As she scrubbed its back and underbelly, front legs and back legs, Ana held on to the goat by its collar. It bleated mournfully.

"You're okay," Rebecca said, trying to comfort the little goat. She wished she could say the same about Ollie. Even if she mended quickly, what would stop someone from trying to hurt her again?

"Ana," she said, setting down her brush. "We need to talk about our friend Ollie."

"*Your* friend," Ana said, not meeting Rebecca's eyes. "She did not act like my friend today. Yelling at me about ice bucket. She act like she is queen or something."

"She *is* something, Ana! She landed a headline role with the Ziegfeld Follies, and that's not an easy thing to do." Rebecca looked her cousin in the eye. "Ana, you don't understand. Someone tampered with her swing."

"Tamper? Means what?"

Rebecca hopped up and grabbed a clump of clean straw in her wet hands. She gathered several golden pieces together, then broke most in half, leaving only a few pieces intact. "Someone cut the cable and left just a few strands of wire, knowing they would hold only for a moment and then break under Ollie's weight." She dropped the straw.

A cloud of concern passed over Ana's face. "Bubbie was right," she said, shaking her head. "This vaudeville is not good. I think we quit."

"We *can't* quit," Rebecca reminded her. "Mr. Hammerstein wants us to tell him what's happening at the Victory—and your brother needs his job."

Ana said nothing as she hosed off the goat. Rebecca caught the next goat, carried it to the tub, and plopped it in the suds. Just then, a long shadow crossed the metal tub. Rebecca glanced up and dropped the scrub brush. "Oh, Mr. Hammerstein!"

"These little ones caused a heap of trouble last evening," he said.

Ana winced, as if expecting a scolding. "Now goats cannot get out," she offered. "No more problems."

Mr. Hammerstein grinned. "Performers need to have some spirit! Some spunk! Regular circus act they are. Got right onstage and stole the show! They had the audience rolling in the aisles!"

"You're not mad?" Rebecca asked.

"No," Mr. Hammerstein said. "But I am glad to see they're contained now. It's better to plan performances than to be surprised." The wet baby goat Rebecca was holding shook its coat, sending a spray of water onto Mr. Hammerstein's suit coat. He brushed the droplets off and continued. "Speaking of surprises, I don't want any more. What do you have to report from your visit to the New Amsterdam today?"

Rebecca tightened her grip on the baby goat that writhed in her arms. She felt just as trapped by Mr. Hammerstein. If she said too much about Ollie, she was betraying her friend. If she said nothing, she was risking her own job—and Ana's, and even Michael's. Mr. Hammerstein had made that clear.

She thought for a moment. Telling him the truth, that Ollie had fallen, might take some of the pressure off. If the New Amsterdam's star performer wasn't in tip-top shape, he might worry less about competition from the theater. Maybe he wouldn't press the girls so hard for information. It probably couldn't make things worse, anyway.

"Mr. Hammerstein," she said, "something terrible happened to Olivia Berry today."

He found a cigar in his pocket, lit it, and puffed. "Terrible, you say?"

She gave him the whole story, including the part about the mysterious way the wire cable had been cut, leaving a few strands that would easily snap. "No matter how she's feeling, though," Rebecca couldn't help adding, "she says the show will go on."

"I see," he said with a shrug. "That's it for today?"

Without waiting for a reply, he turned and strode away. Rebecca picked up her soapy brush and began working on the goat's spindly legs. "Ana, I don't understand. The lead star of his rival show could have been killed. Yet he didn't seem to care!"

"Maybe is regular day in show business," Ana replied, rinsing the last soapy, wiggling goat as it bleated in complaint.

Rebecca knew that Mr. Hammerstein and Mr. Ziegfeld were archrivals. A dark thought crossed her mind. *What if the news of Ollie's fall really isn't news at all to Mr. Hammerstein?* What if he wasn't surprised because *he* was the one who was responsible? Was this the "drastic action" he'd spoken of earlier?

It was difficult for Rebecca to believe that Mr. Hammerstein would go so far as to try to hurt Ollie physically. But he was a man who stole furniture from a ship and had no problem tricking customers to get more money from them. If his tricks included sabotaging a competitor's act, then she and Ana had just informed him that his scheme had failed.

The freshly rinsed goat shook its coat, sending water everywhere. Rebecca wiped the droplets from her face, wishing she could as easily sweep away her growing concern for Ollie.

The next morning, Rebecca found it hard to think of anything except how to help keep Ollie safe. After everything that had happened, cleaning out a chicken coop seemed like a terrible waste of time. But with rain falling steadily, at least she and Ana would be able to work indoors and stay dry. As the girls swept down cobwebs, the chickens huddled under a small tin roof in their barnyard for shelter. The girls freshened boxes with new straw, shoveled the floor clean, and managed to finish before lunch. They washed up in the barn, gobbled their food like hungry chickens, and hurried to the New Amsterdam with the glass of milk Flora had set aside.

As they walked down the long hallway to the dressing rooms, the girls passed an alcove in which four Ziegfeld Girls were sprawled in overstuffed chairs.

"We're supposed to postpone rehearsal simply because *she's* having a hard time?" one of the women huffed.

Another threw up her hands. "You don't know what I went through to get here on time today!"

"And now we twiddle our thumbs till she feels better," Tilly Parker said. She jabbed the air with her cigarette holder.

Rebecca caught Tilly's eye as she hurried past, and the woman crossed her arms. "Huh. There goes her little sister, delivering her precious beauty milk again."

"I'm going to go stretch," another woman said, her voice fading as Rebecca and Ana moved on. "I can't sit around here all day."

Rebecca quickened her pace, with Ana at her heels. Something felt wrong. Ollie's fall onstage must have been worse than it seemed.

They found Ollie slumped at her dressing table. The mirror reflected a face that didn't look like Ollie's at all—splotchy patches of skin surrounded sunken, tear-filled eyes. The edges of her nostrils were red. She grabbed a handkerchief and blew loudly.

Rebecca hurried to her side. She placed the glass of milk on the dressing table, then knelt beside Ollie's chair. "What's wrong, Ollie?"

Ollie's sobs came in great gulps. When she caught her breath, she met Rebecca's eyes and

continued in a whisper. "I got here early and, and . . .
he was just lying there."

"Who? Mr. Ziegfeld?" Rebecca asked, horrified.

"Nooo. Sweetie. He was at the bottom of his cage.
When I picked him up, his little body was as still as
a stone. Light as a feather. And I knew . . ." Ollie bent
her head into her hands.

Tears spilled down Rebecca's cheeks. "Poor
Sweetie! Oh, Ollie, I'm so sorry!"

"He was nice bird," Ana said, drawing closer.
She sat down and leaned her head into Rebecca's
shoulder.

"I was just getting to know him," Ollie said,
wiping her eyes. "It's so strange. Yesterday afternoon when I left him, he seemed perfectly healthy.
Ziggy says maybe it was too much change for a bird.
Maybe his little heart just gave out . . ."

She straightened and turned back to the mirror.
She poured water from a ceramic pitcher into
a matching basin, wet a washcloth, and held it to

her face. The girls waited beside her. Ollie's shoulders rose and fell, rose and fell. Time slowed, and Rebecca turned away. *That's one bad thing about being a star,* she realized. *You can't fall apart without everyone knowing it.*

Ana looked to Rebecca and mouthed silently, "Let's go."

Rebecca mouthed back, "Wait."

Finally, Ollie removed the cloth and nodded to herself in the mirror. "Okay. That's enough. I need to pull myself together and move on." She took a long drink of milk as a knock sounded at the door.

"Special delivery for Miss Berry," came a voice.

"Get that, will you?" Ollie asked.

Rebecca opened the door to a young man holding a bouquet of roses. An explosion of deep red buds on long stems fanned above his head like a torch. "For Miss Berry."

"Thank you," Rebecca said. "I'll see that she gets these." Rebecca placed the flowers on a table beside the chaise, then pulled out the attached card and held it out to Ollie.

"If it's not from Ziggy, I don't care," Ollie said, dabbing beige makeup under her eyes. "If you're curious, go ahead and read it."

From the white card, Rebecca read aloud:

> *"Sorry for your loss.*
> *Know that you are loved by many,*
> *including me.*
> *Devotedly yours, F."*

"Who's it from?" Rebecca asked.

"Oh, just another fan," Ollie said as she took up a tiny brush and used it to darken her brows.

When the girls left the theater, Frank greeted them and pulled an envelope from his jacket and held it out to Ana. "Ladies! Please give this to

Flora," he said. "Make sure she gets it."

"We will," Ana said, taking the envelope.

When they held the envelope out to Flora in the barn, her face lit up. She tore open the envelope, unfolded the note, and began to read it eagerly. But as she read, her smile disappeared. Her brows gathered together. She let the note drop to the floor and pressed her fingers against her trembling lower lip.

"Bad news?" Ana whispered.

Flora's voice came out raspy and threadbare. "He says he needs more time. He won't agree to marrying sooner. He won't agree to any date yet at all."

"I'm sorry," Ana said.

"Me too," Rebecca added. She bent to pick up Flora's letter. The handwriting on the message looked familiar. Rebecca caught her breath. It was in the same script as the one just delivered to Ollie! The note was even signed exactly the same way:

Devotedly yours, F.

The realization hit Rebecca like a slap: *F.* was Frank! Suddenly his nearly tearful reaction to the news of Ollie's accident made new sense. Frank was in love with her! No wonder he resisted setting a date to marry Flora. He was hoping to win Ollie over. As Rebecca handed the note back to Flora, it almost seemed to burn in her fingers.

The expression on Flora's face had darkened. Her next words were bitter and hard. "I'll bet you anything *she's* behind it," she said.

"Who?" Ana asked innocently. Rebecca shot her a warning look.

"Miss Olivia Berry." Flora practically spat out her name. "It wouldn't be the first time she stole someone from me! Not so long ago, she and I worked at the same department store. My old boyfriend used to visit me there. Then Ollie turned on her charms, and sure enough, he was done with me. Now she's turned up next door with the Follies. And now Frank—"

Rebecca's face grew hot. Against her better judgment, she rose to Ollie's defense. "She couldn't help it if—"

"That woman's a curse!" Flora shouted. "I want her out of my life!"

The words felt like a knife in Rebecca's chest.

chapter 9

A Cornered Animal

SHAKEN, THE GIRLS finished their chores in silence to avoid prompting another outburst from Flora. At the end of the day, keeping an eye out for rats, they headed down the stairs for their daily visit with Mr. Hammerstein.

"I feel terrible," Ana whispered, following close on Rebecca's heels. "Ollie is breaking Flora's heart."

"I feel bad for Flora, too," Rebecca said. "But it's not Ollie who's breaking her heart—at least not on purpose. And maybe it's better in the long run." She paused. "Ana, there's something you don't know."

Ana stopped midstep. "What?"

Rebecca turned to face her on the stairs. "When I picked up Frank's note to Flora, I noticed that the handwriting on the letter was exactly the same as the handwriting in the note that came with the roses to Ollie's dressing room. Both were signed 'Devotedly yours, F.' Both of those notes were written by Frank, Ana. *He's* the one chasing Ollie, not the other way around."

"Then we must tell Flora," Ana declared. "Is right for her to know." She turned on the steps to begin climbing back up, but Rebecca grabbed her hand.

"Ana! You can't!" she said. "She won't ever believe it isn't Ollie's fault. Telling her that her own fiancé gave roses to Ollie would ... would ..." She paused and drew in a deep breath. "You saw how angry she was. You heard what she said. Who knows what she would do? She might—"

Rebecca stopped midsentence. As angry as Flora was at Ollie, Rebecca realized, she might *already* have tried to hurt Ollie.

"I wouldn't be surprised if she was the one who cut the swing's cable," Rebecca said to Ana. "She said she wanted Ollie out of her life."

"Was only talk," Ana said. "She is like hurt animal in corner."

That, Rebecca thought grimly, *is when an animal is most dangerous.*

"But Ollie doesn't love Frank," Rebecca tried to explain. "She didn't even want to read his note. She's in love with Mr. Ziegfeld. She's pretty, and so many men fall in love with her. Ollie can't help what her fans do."

"She has enough fans," Ana said. "I feel bad for Flora. And is terrible thing to think she would hurt Ollie."

It *was* terrible, Rebecca thought. But that didn't mean it wasn't true.

Rounding the last landing, Rebecca wondered whether she'd been wrong to think Mr. Hammerstein had anything to do with hurting Ollie. The only people who had said anything threatening about her were Tilly—and now Flora. Still, Rebecca felt awful telling Mr. Hammerstein anything more about Ollie. She forced her footsteps toward his office, glad, at least, that because there had been no rehearsal at the New Amsterdam, they had nothing to report.

"What's the news, girls?" Mr. Hammerstein said when they entered his office. He glanced up from an array of papers and fixed Ana and Rebecca with a penetrating stare.

"We don't have any news about the show," Rebecca said. "Rehearsal was postponed today."

He cocked his head. "Certainly there must have been a reason. Was someone sick?"

Rebecca hesitated. If she told Mr. Hammerstein about Sweetie's death, could he use it against Ollie somehow? It didn't seem likely. "Not sick, exactly—" she began.

"Be clear, girl!" Mr. Hammerstein barked. "Don't forget what I'm paying you for!"

"It's just . . ." Rebecca swallowed before going on. "Miss Berry was in an awful way. Her new pet cockatoo, Sweetie, died!"

"Interesting." Mr. Hammerstein opened a desk

drawer and removed a case. He selected a cigar from the case and rolled it slowly between his fingers. A half smile came to his lips. "Interesting that such a little mishap can stop a big show in its tracks."

"Yes, sir," Rebecca replied, unsure how to read his response.

"Okay, go on then," he said, striking a match. "Keep up the good work."

The girls left the theater and waited in silence outside for Michael. Nothing about the day, Rebecca thought, had been good at all.

The girls sat in silence on the clattering subway ride home.

Michael looked from Ana to Rebecca. "Why you girls so quiet?" Michael asked. "Most days you talk with no stopping until we are home."

Rebecca gave him a weary smile. "I guess you could say that we had a long day at work."

Michael nodded, but Ana wouldn't meet Rebecca's eyes—and Rebecca didn't have to ask why. They were at odds about whether to tell Flora about Frank's disloyalty—and about whether Flora might have tried to hurt Ollie. But because Flora was Ana's friend, just like Ollie was Rebecca's friend, Rebecca knew there was probably no way to make Ana understand, or share, her misgivings.

As the cousins exited the train, trudged up the subway stairs, and began the silent walk home, the long, awful day replayed in Rebecca's head:

The Ziegfeld Girls snickering in the hallway.

Sweetie's death.

Ollie's anguish.

Flora's fury.

And Mr. Hammerstein's horrible half smile when Rebecca had finished her report. His last words repeated in her head: *Interesting that such a little mishap can stop a big show in its tracks.* Just as before, he hadn't seemed at all surprised by the news that

Sweetie's death had brought Ziegfeld's rehearsal to a halt. In fact, Rebecca thought, he'd seemed pleased. Then another thought struck. Rebecca nearly tripped but caught herself just in time.

What if it wasn't just one person who was to blame for the broken swing and Sweetie's death? Mr. Hammerstein was used to ordering people around. He could have ordered someone else to do his dirty work—to cut the swing's cable and hurt Sweetie. He could have forced them, just the way he'd sent her and Ana to do his spying. *Or,* Rebecca thought grimly, *someone might be angry enough at Ollie to do it without being forced. Someone like Flora.*

Flora, Rebecca reasoned, would be as able as anyone to cause trouble at Ziegfeld's theater. Her fiancé was the doorman. He kept other people out of the theater, but he'd certainly let Flora in anytime she asked.

Rebecca drew a sharp breath. If she was right that Mr. Hammerstein and Flora were conspiring, it was likely that another "accident" would happen soon. After all, he still hadn't stopped the upcoming show, and opening night was just two days away.

By the time the three cousins had reached Rebecca's family's apartment building, Rebecca had decided two things: Starting tomorrow, she would keep an extra close eye on Flora. And when the girls made their midday milk delivery, Rebecca would insist that Ollie take her warnings seriously.

Ollie's life depended on it.

chapter 10

Loneliest Girl
in New York

THE NEXT MORNING, Ana was still distant, so once the girls climbed from the subway into the light of day, Rebecca stepped alongside Michael for the half-block walk to the Victory. She wanted to ask him a question.

"Michael, is there anyone who works for Mr. Hammerstein—besides Flora—who might dislike Olivia Berry enough to hurt her?"

The question seemed to catch him off guard. "Why anyone want to hurt her? Everyone is big fan. Just look at my boss."

"Yes, Mr. O'Hara does seem quite infatuated with her."

"Infatuated." Michael wrinkled his nose. "What is this word?"

134

"In love."

Michael laughed. "Mr. O'Hara! Yes. One time, I see him on street and he defend her."

"Defend her? From who?" Rebecca asked, hoping it might offer a clue about who wanted to harm Ollie.

"A fan—a man keep asking for kiss."

"What did Mr. O'Hara do?" Ana asked.

Michael smiled, as if proud of his boss. "He grabbed the man and said, 'You'll be leavin' Miss Berry alone or you'll be kissin' this.'" Michael raised his fist, imitating Mr. O'Hara, and chuckled. "End of problem."

Hurrying up the stairs to the rooftop, Rebecca wished Ollie's current problems could be solved as swiftly. But if Mr. Hammerstein really was behind the whole thing, a set painter like Mr. O'Hara would be powerless to stop him.

•••

Although Rebecca hurried through her chores, she and Ana were running late when they reached Ollie's dressing room during their lunch break. They found the door open a crack. From inside came the sounds of clattering and banging.

Rebecca met Ana's questioning eyes. What was happening in Ollie's dressing room? They edged closer to the door. Leaning around the frame, Rebecca peeked in.

Inside was one of the Ziegfeld Girls, her star-spangled costume shimmering in the light of Ollie's vanity. Rebecca caught a glimpse of the woman's face in the mirror: Tilly Parker. She was yanking open one drawer after another, rifling through their contents, then slamming them shut. She was clearly looking for something.

Rebecca stepped boldly into the doorway. "What are you doing here?" she demanded. She didn't try to hide the tone of accusation in her voice.

Tilly pivoted in her high heels, clutching a small

box in her hand. "Oh!" Tilly said. "You startled me."

"Where's Ollie?" Rebecca asked, eyeing the little container.

"She just fainted offstage!" Tilly exclaimed. "She needs her smelling salts." She shook the little box in her hand. "One of the gals said she's been using them lately to fend off dizzy spells. Now if you'll excuse me." She hurried with the container past the girls.

Her mind spinning, Rebecca set the glass of milk on the dressing table, and then rushed to the door that led backstage, with Ana close behind. From the stage came the rhythmic swish of Will Rogers's rope and the sound of his voice rising and falling as he rehearsed his jokes. Rebecca stood tall, reminded herself to act like Ollie's sister, and stepped backstage, holding Ana's hand.

Ollie lay on the floor, the silky blue fabric of her dress spread around her like a cloud. Tilly squatted beside her, holding the small box beneath Ollie's nose. Suddenly, Ollie jolted awake. She looked around, as if trying to figure out where she was, and pushed up to her elbows.

"Don't stand up right away," Tilly said.

Ollie stood anyway. "I'm on next," she said weakly.

Mr. Ziegfeld rushed in, catching Ollie as she started to wobble. She collapsed in his arms, started coughing, and then clapped her hand to her mouth as if she were about to become very sick.

"Oh, Ollie!" Rebecca said. Feeling powerless to help, she turned to Ana, who pulled her into a hug.

"No stage for you today, Ollie. Let's get you home," said Mr. Ziegfeld. He motioned to Rebecca and Ana. "Go home with your sister. I'll send the doctor to look in on her at her apartment."

Before Rebecca could say a word, Mr. Ziegfeld was ushering the girls down the hall toward the exit as a stagehand carried Ollie in his arms ahead of them.

"Frank," Mr. Ziegfeld said as they pushed

through the door, "get her a cab to take her to her apartment."

"Of course, Mr. Ziegfeld," Frank said. His eyes flashed with fear as he stepped into the street and blew a whistle on a cord around his neck. When a cab pulled alongside the curb, Frank helped Ollie into the cab and handed the driver a dollar.

"Stay with her until the doctor arrives," he told Rebecca, nearly pushing her into the cab after Ollie.

Ana held back. "I'll let Flora know what's happened and where you've gone."

Rebecca nodded. But as the cab sped away, she wished she could stop Ana from telling Flora anything at all. Who knew what Flora might do with the information?

The cab driver wound through street after street, arriving at a brownstone building on the edge of Central Park. When the doorman stepped down and opened their cab door, Rebecca slid out first, then helped Ollie from the cab, up the red stone steps past pots of blooming flowers, and into her apartment on the second floor.

Once inside, Ollie sank into a blue velvet sofa, and Rebecca covered her with a soft pink blanket she found draped on the sofa's arm. Ollie reached up and squeezed her hand. "I'm glad you're here," she said.

"Me, too," Rebecca replied.

When Ollie's eyelids closed, Rebecca took a moment to look around. The apartment was modest, but well-kept. There were a few small paintings decorating the walls, a tidy little fireplace, and a large window that let in the golden sunlight.

In the small kitchen, Rebecca made a pot of tea, found crackers and put them on a plate, and returned with a tray to the living room. But Ollie was already asleep.

Rebecca set down the tray on a nearby table, and picked up one of several magazines featuring Olivia Berry on their covers. She thumbed to an article about Ollie's meteoric rise to the most recognizable face in New York City.

Curious, Rebecca scanned the text. When she got to a passage about Ollie's humble beginnings as Olivia Kelly, an Irish immigrant child in a "smoke-choked coal mining town in Pennsylvania," she set down the magazine. *Of course!* The other day when Ollie had talked to Ana about girls who'd worked hard to lose their accents, she'd been talking about *herself*! Rebecca shook her head in wonder. It was hard to change your way of speaking as dramatically as Ollie must have. She was an even better performer than Rebecca had thought.

Ollie moaned, and Rebecca looked up. She set down the magazine and laid the back of her hand lightly on Ollie's forehead. It was hot. "The doctor should be here soon," she said.

"Mmm," was all Ollie said.

Another half hour passed before the doctor finally arrived, black satchel in hand. When he began asking

Ollie personal questions, Rebecca decided to step into the hallway to give Ollie her privacy. After what seemed like a very long time, the doctor emerged from the apartment, clicking his bag shut. "See that she drinks plenty of water and tea," he said, his tone hushed. "And see that she rests. Since you're her sister, I should tell you ..."

Rebecca bit her lip. She wanted to tell the doctor the truth that she wasn't Ollie's sister. If he had some dreadful news, she wasn't the person to tell. Surely Ollie had real family somewhere who belonged with her at such a time. But no one was there. And Rebecca genuinely cared.

"What is it?" Rebecca whispered back.

"Whatever Miss Berry is suffering from seems far more serious than a common cold," he said. "I've drawn some blood, and I'm going to conduct a few tests when I return to my office."

"Tests?" Rebecca asked. "That does sound serious."

The doctor nodded. "I will know more later," he

said, and started down the stairs.

Rebecca turned the doorknob slowly, taking care not to wake Ollie if she'd drifted back to sleep. She hoped the doctor would finish his tests quickly and that he'd be able to help Ollie. Sooner rather than later.

Ollie's eyes were closed. Gathering up the teapot, Rebecca went to the kitchen to make a fresh pot. When she returned, Ollie was sitting with the blanket around her shoulders, her feet tucked under her on the sofa. She patted the space beside her. "Sit with me," she said weakly.

Together they drank tea from delicate porcelain cups and ate crackers. It reminded Rebecca of the times when she'd been sick and Mama had been there with a comforting word or a cup of broth. "Ollie," she said, "do you have any family nearby? Anybody who can help you when you're not feeling well?"

Ollie closed her eyes for a moment, then opened them. "No," she said. Tears budded at the base of her long lashes. "Sometimes, Beckie, I think I won the award for the Loneliest Girl in New York. Even before I won that shopgirl competition, it was hard to have close friends. The people in the town where I grew up didn't understand my dreams of becoming an actress. They came from one county in Ireland and knew only one way of life. I was determined to use my talents to rise up. And you know what?"

"What?" Rebecca said, eager to learn all she could about Ollie and her path to success.

"People don't like that," Ollie told her. "They don't want you to grow and move beyond them. They want you to stay where—and who—you are. My parents wanted to hang on to the old ways and customs from Ireland, but I have only ever wanted to be American." Abruptly, Ollie switched to an Irish accent. *"Aye, but I say there's more to life than mutton stew with potatoes an' onions. What d'ye say?"*

"I say you really are Irish!" Rebecca replied.

"Only by birth, baby doll," Ollie said, instantly shifting her speech back. "I'm more myself now than

I've ever been. This is who I am. And I aim to see just how far I can go. I'm learning to dance, and I hope to break into the movie business before long. I have a whole career ahead of me—if I can stay well."

She leaned her head against the back of the sofa. "Oh, my stomach's killing me. Ziggy thinks I might be pushing too hard, but if I don't, some other gal will fill my shoes on that stage. That's what all the other girls want."

"I never thought being ambitious could be bad," Rebecca said, thinking of how fervently she wished to be onstage.

"Ambition's not a bad thing," Ollie countered. Then her expression turned dark. "Unless you trample people to get where you're going."

Rebecca studied Ollie's pale face. Who wanted to be in her spot more than anything? Who would trample her to get star billing? Tilly Parker, that's who. Despite her growing suspicions about Flora and Mr. Hammerstein, Rebecca realized she couldn't rule out Tilly. Tilly had been rummaging around in Ollie's room earlier today. Were the smelling salts only an excuse? It wasn't as if Tilly was inclined to help Ollie, after all. Tilly had wanted to see her "break a leg—or worse."

"I think Tilly Parker might try to trample anyone who got in her way," Rebecca said at last.

Ollie shrugged. "I think her bark is worse than her bite. But when it comes to being onstage, feelings run high, I'll grant you that." She sipped her tea, added another lump of sugar, and stirred it with a tiny silver spoon. When she took another sip, she smiled weakly. "The tea seems to help a bit."

On- or offstage, Rebecca thought, envy seemed a very sharp dagger. "Tilly Parker never has anything good to say about you," she said. "You know, when I arrived today, she was in your room."

"In my room?" Ollie frowned.

"She said she was looking for smelling salts," Rebecca added.

"I suppose I needed them."

"I'm worried for you, Ollie," Rebecca said. "I don't think you should return to the theater."

"Oh, that's ridiculous," Ollie replied. "Why wouldn't I?"

"If someone's trying to hurt you, it's not worth the risk. I would hate to see anything happen to my big sister."

"Look." Ollie set down her teacup, and her face grew stern. "I know you mean well, but I'm an actress. And no matter what, the show must go on."

Ollie reached for her beaded purse, pulled out a dollar bill, and pressed it into Rebecca's palm. "For a cab back to the Victory. It's nearing the end of your workday. I don't want you to be late getting home." She motioned with the curve of her finger to come closer. Rebecca did so, and Ollie planted a kiss on her cheek.

"Thanks for caring, sis," Ollie said. "You're a keeper."

Rebecca took the teapot to the kitchen, then let herself out of the apartment, glancing back before she pulled the door shut. Ollie was already slumped on the sofa, her hand pressed to her stomach, her eyes closed in pain.

chapter 11
Setting a Trap

ON THE SUBWAY ride home that night, both
the girls were quiet. As they walked up the street
toward her family's apartment building, Rebecca
could not bear the silence a second longer. She leaned
close to her cousin and spoke softly. "Ana, I'm worried, and I really need to talk to you," she said. "Can
you stay at our apartment tonight?"

"All right," Ana said. It was the best thing Rebecca
had heard all day. They waved good-bye to Michael,
who promised to tell Uncle Jacob that Ana would stay
with Rebecca's family for the night, and stepped into
the apartment. Rebecca breathed a sigh of relief. She
was home—and safe.

After washing dishes together, and after visiting
upstairs with Bubbie and Grandpa, the girls stepped

149

out onto the fire escape to clean their work uniforms in a washtub.

They were silent for a moment as they scrubbed the knees of their overalls, enjoying the cool air rushing up the side of the building from the alleyway. As Rebecca went over the horrible day in her head, she felt as if she would burst with emotion.

"Ana," Rebecca said at last, looking up from a particularly stubborn stain. She bit her bottom lip as tears pooled in her eyes.

"Mmm?" Ana said, glancing at her cousin. She set her uniform aside as tears began streaming down Rebecca's cheeks.

Rebecca told her cousin all about her time with Ollie and how lonely she had seemed. And she shared what the doctor had told her about conducting tests.

After a moment, Ana spoke. "Maybe is show biz that makes Ollie sick."

"She does push herself very hard," Rebecca said,

using the sleeve of her nightgown to wipe her wet face. She explained what she'd learned about Ollie's background as an immigrant, and how hard she'd worked to become an American and shed her Irish accent.

"I am proud to be American," Ana said. "But why is bad if people know I am from Russia when I speak?"

"It's not, Ana," Rebecca said, putting her hand on her cousin's. "It's just something Ollie wanted to change—for herself."

Ana exhaled slowly. "I will try to understand. Ollie is your friend." She paused. "But Flora is my friend. She would not hurt Ollie. I know this."

Rebecca hated being at odds with Ana so much that she almost agreed. Instead, she said, "Ana, I just want Ollie to be safe. If you are sure Flora didn't hurt her, will you help me find out who did?"

"I will," Ana said. Then she yawned.

Rebecca yawned in agreement. "We should get ready for bed. We have a big day ahead of us at work tomorrow." As they pinned their clean uniforms to the clothesline, she felt incredibly grateful that she and Ana had found better footing.

Before returning inside, Ana said, "Any more bad things happen, you tell me, yes?"

"I will. Thank you, Ana."

When Friday dawned, the girls quickly ate their breakfast, grabbed rolls and cheese for lunch, and then headed out the door in their work uniforms. Throughout the morning on the rooftop, Rebecca kept a close eye on Flora. She seemed heartbroken over Frank's note, but not particularly agitated or resentful.

When midday arrived and the girls delivered milk to Ollie's dressing room, they found the door ajar and the room empty. Rebecca's heart sank. Was Ollie still too ill to work? She set the glass carefully on the dresser and left the room with Ana.

"Let's check the stage," she said. "They might

have started rehearsal early to make up for yesterday." Rebecca didn't think it was likely. Still, it was
better than pacing in Ollie's empty room, worrying
about her.

As the girls hurried down the hall, they crossed
paths with Tilly Parker, who flashed them a resentful
glare as she sashayed by in her dressing gown.

Rebecca took Ana's hand and hustled ahead. If
Ollie *was* somewhere in the theater, Rebecca didn't
want to leave her alone with Tilly.

But when the girls entered the theater, neither
Ollie nor any of the performers were there. The stage
was dark, except for the faint glow of the small ghost
light that kept the stage safe when the main lights
weren't on.

"Hmmm." Rebecca hesitated for a few moments
at the back of the theater. "I guess we should go back
and wait for Ollie in her dressing room. Maybe she's
running late because she was so sick yesterday."

Relief flooded through Rebecca when they

returned and found Ollie in front of her mirror, intently applying makeup over the dark circles under her eyes. "Hello, girls," she said, looking up. Her voice sounded tired. "I was just up in Ziggy's office. He's offered to get me another bird. But I don't know." She smoothed in the foundation with a small sponge, then dabbed rouge on her cheeks with a small brush. "Maybe this just isn't the place for such a tender little creature—"

She was interrupted by a quiet knock at the door. "Excuse me," came a low voice. "Miss Berry? It's Dr. Schneider, here to see you."

Ollie motioned to Rebecca to open the door.

"Hello, Doctor," Rebecca said, letting him in. She closed the door behind him.

"Miss Berry, how are you feeling today?" he asked.

"Much better, thank you," Ollie said with a radiant smile. "I'm sure I just needed some rest."

The doctor nodded gravely. "A word in private, please?" he asked.

She shook her head. "No, the girls can stay. Tell me what you think is going on. Why did I get so sick yesterday? I need to get better—and fast."

The doctor met Ollie's pleading gaze. "I'll be direct. My tests indicate that you have consumed arsenic. It is a poison."

Rebecca's breathing stopped.

"Poison?" Ollie said, wrapping her arms tightly around herself. Despite her makeup, her face lost a shade of color. "But how?"

"Either you have been exposed to it accidentally, or . . ." he paused a moment, "someone is trying to make you sick."

"Oh dear!" Ollie exclaimed.

"It wasn't a huge dose, thankfully," the doctor went on. "Nowhere near lethal, at least not for a human. A smaller creature, like a rat or a cat, would have fared far worse."

Or a bird? Rebecca cast a glance at Sweetie's cage. The sight of it empty filled her with sudden sadness.

She missed Sweetie's chatter and antics, how he'd called everyone "pretty baby" and poked his head into Ollie's milk when she wasn't looking. And Ollie had loved him.

Suddenly, Rebecca froze. Ollie and Sweetie had both consumed the milk! Had the milk been *poisoned*? It was almost unbearable to think that something she'd been bringing to Ollie might have been used to hurt her.

Ollie was reaching for the glass on her dressing table. Rebecca snatched it away.

"What?" Ollie said with a tired laugh. "You're not going to let me have my beauty milk? I need it today more than ever."

"Ollie," Rebecca's voice was grave, "do you remember when Sweetie took a drink of your milk?"

"Of course! He was so cute ..." Imitating Sweetie, she tipped her nose down, then lifted it to the sky, pretending to swallow. "It was—oh no—right before he died!" Her shoulders drooped, and her hands went to her face. "Is milk bad for birds?"

Maybe not milk, Rebecca thought, *but what was in the milk.* She leaned away from the glass in her hand, as if just holding it could make her sick. "Doctor, if someone poisoned the milk—meant for Ollie—and if her cockatoo took a few sips, it could kill him, right?"

"Most certainly," the doctor said. "Birds are especially fragile."

"Where would someone get their hands on arsenic?" Ollie asked.

"Arsenic is more common than you'd guess," the doctor said. "I've seen poisonings aplenty—mostly children getting into rat poison by mistake. Arsenic is the main ingredient in rat poison, and it's used all around the city."

"Heaven knows we have our share of rats here in the theater," Ollie said.

Rebecca shuddered, thinking of the rats in the stairwells at Mr. Hammerstein's theater. For a moment, silence settled in the dressing room.

"Now what will I do?" Ollie asked plaintively. "I have to eat!"

"In Russia," Ana said, "someone has job of tasting food for the czar. They must taste every food and drink before Czar Nicholas can eat it, to be safe."

Ollie half-smiled at Ana. "Just what I need. A food taster. Somehow, I think that will be a tough job to fill."

"I wish I had better news," the doctor said. "For now, I want to check your pulse and examine your eyes. And, Miss Berry, you must alert the police. The person who did this must be found."

Ollie's head dropped into her hands. "Girls, I guess I don't really care for any milk today."

Rebecca nodded. She wouldn't want milk either. "I'll dump it out," she said, and headed for the door. Ana followed.

But by the time they had made it halfway down the hallway, Rebecca had changed her mind. She would not throw out the milk. At least not yet. "Tilly Parker," she whispered to Ana. "Any time we leave the milk in Ollie's room, Tilly could be putting poison in it. We left the milk on the dressing table on Tuesday and Wednesday, the day before Ollie got sick. And just a moment ago, Tilly was headed in the direction of Ollie's dressing room. She could have poisoned this very glass! Let's go find her."

"And do what?" Ana whispered. "Ollie must call police."

Rebecca shook her head. "She won't. I know she won't."

"Why?"

"Because she won't want to stir up any trouble, especially if it's coming from another performer. I think I have an idea for how to trap Tilly into confessing."

Rebecca hurried directly to the stage. A few dancers were there now, stretching. The orchestra was warming up.

"Is bad idea," Ana whispered, tugging at Rebecca's overall strap.

"She's back there," Rebecca said, recognizing Tilly's star-spangled outfit at the right side of the stage. Ignoring Ana, she forced herself toward the shimmery sequins, head high as if she belonged onstage, and tapped Tilly on the back.

"Oh, you," Tilly said, turning from the other dancer she'd been speaking with. "What is it now? Did she faint *again*?"

In answer, Rebecca held out the glass of milk.

"What am I supposed to do with this?" Tilly asked, tilting her chin in the air snidely.

"Ollie wants you to have this," Rebecca lied. "She wanted to thank you for helping her yesterday."

Tilly shrugged her bare shoulders. "Well, I didn't do much. Who wouldn't help her? She just dropped like rag doll." She accepted the glass and eyed it suspiciously. "If Ollie's sick, I don't want to catch what she's got. She hasn't drunk from it, has she?"

"No," Rebecca answered. That, at least, was true. She turned and flashed a knowing look at Ana. Tilly had behaved just as Rebecca had suspected she would. If Tilly had poisoned Ollie's milk, no amount of prodding would get her to drink it now.

But when Rebecca turned back to confront Tilly, the dancer had already brought the glass to her lips and begun to drink!

"No!" Rebecca snatched the glass from Tilly's hands. Milk sloshed onto Tilly's wrist, and onto the stage floor.

"Why'd you go and do that?" Tilly asked, brushing droplets of milk from her costume.

Rebecca swallowed hard. What *had* she done? If the doctor had been right, the one or two swallows Tilly had managed to drink wouldn't be enough to make her ill. But there was no question: She had to tell Tilly anyway.

"I'm sorry," Rebecca said, squeezing out the words around the lump that had formed in her throat. "The milk might be poisoned. I didn't think you would drink it. It probably won't make you sick, but you should see Dr. Schneider just in case."

With a look of horror, Tilly clasped her hands to her mouth and ran from the stage.

chapter 12
Into the Darkness

THE GIRLS HURRIED out of the New Amsterdam, and Rebecca poured what was left of the milk into the sewer. "Good riddance!" she said. As they climbed the stairs to the rooftop garden, she thought about what to do next. If arsenic was used to get rid of rats, there was probably no shortage of the poison at the Victory Theater. There were rats everywhere. And the person who was using rat poison to make Ollie sick could be someone she and her cousin saw there every day.

"Ana," she whispered. "There are only two people left who could be out to hurt Ollie."

"Who?"

"The first is Mr. Hammerstein."

Ana shook her head. "Not him. He cannot sneak

in New Amsterdam Theater. Everyone knows him. That is why he sends us to spy for him."

"That's true." Rebecca paused on the second-floor landing. "But he could have ordered someone else to add poison to the milk. Someone who works for him."

"Like who?" Ana said. A note of resistance had crept into her voice.

A skittering movement caught Rebecca's attention. She flinched as a rat passed them on the landing, darted down a few steps, and disappeared into a crevice in the wall.

"There's more than one kind of rat in the world," Rebecca said, crossing her arms and rubbing her hands up and down them to chase away a sudden chill. She hurried up the last two flights of stairs and stopped before opening the door to the rooftop. Facing Ana, she whispered, "Ana, I don't want to start an argument all over again, but only one person has constant access to Ollie's milk: Flora."

"Is not possible." Ana's tone was adamant. "Lots of people work for Mr. Hammerstein. It could be anybody else, but not Flora."

"Then who?"

"Well . . ." Ana floundered. "I know only Mr. O'Hara."

"That's nonsense," Rebecca said, more harshly than she meant to. "Mr. O'Hara adores Ollie. Even Flora and Michael say so. He's a very talented set painter. He'd quit and find a new job before going along with that kind of dirty work. Ana, you really have to consider the possibility that Flora might have reason to—"

"No," Ana said. She put her fingers in her ears. "I don't listen." They were both silent a moment before Ana went on. "Rebecca. You say Tilly would not drink milk if she put in poison. The other morning, Flora tasted milk when you said it was bad. That means she did not poison milk."

"Maybe it only *looked* like she tasted it," Rebecca

countered. "Maybe she only smelled it."

Ana's lips tightened into a firm line and she opened the door to the rooftop garden. *Whup, whup, whup* went the windmill as she stomped toward the barn.

"Ana," Rebecca said, catching up with her, "I'm sorry, but too much is at stake. I'm going to ask Flora about the milk."

"Rebecca, please!" Ana cried.

Before losing her resolve, Rebecca strode into the barn with Ana at her heels. She found Flora at the table beneath the window, going over a ledger. Rebecca walked to the table and, surprised at her own boldness, came straight to the point. "Someone is trying to poison Olivia Berry."

"Oh?" Flora crossed her arms. "If it's true, she deserves it."

"How can you say such a thing?" Rebecca asked. She looked at Flora in shock before turning to Ana, who looked just as appalled.

"How do you know someone's trying to poison her?" Flora countered.

Rebecca studied her face. Flora might not have a role on the Victory stage, but she was certainly a good actress. She'd made it seem as if she had nothing to hide.

"Her doctor performed tests," Rebecca replied. "He says Ollie has consumed arsenic—rat poison. And two days ago, her bird, Sweetie, drank from Ollie's glass and died." She waited to see how Flora would respond.

Flora shook her head. "It's too bad about her bird," she said finally. "That stuff is dangerous."

Rebecca squinted at Flora. "That's how the goat died, isn't it? The one we replaced with the babies. You said it got into something it shouldn't have."

"W-well, yes," Flora sputtered. "The poor thing got into one of the rat traps when I was cleaning the goat pen. I didn't want to upset you girls by telling you all the details."

Ana nodded sympathetically but stayed silent.

"So that gave you the idea," Rebecca said. "You poured her milk every day, and you started adding something to it to make her sick."

Flora's jaw dropped in disbelief. "For goodness' sake! Why would I do such a thing?!"

"Because she stole your boyfriend, and now you're worried you'll lose Frank to her," Rebecca insisted. "Because if her opening night is ruined, it might get her out of your life once and for all. But Ollie doesn't *care* about Frank. She loves Mr. Ziegfeld."

Flora gasped. Her eyes flashed dark with anger. "And yet now Frank is postponing our wedding. I know he's under her spell. I can see it," she said, her voice breaking. "Everything was fine between us until Olivia Berry showed up! She ruins everything!" Then she wiped away fresh tears and set her jaw. "Look, I admit that I have no love for Olivia Berry, but that doesn't make me a criminal. And if you girls want to keep working here, you'll drop this silly notion as quickly as it came into your heads. Honestly, I couldn't be more insulted. Now, I'm going to pretend this conversation never happened. If I didn't need help so badly, I'd fire you myself."

Ana looked at her with pleading eyes. "But Flora, I never thought—"

"That's enough," Flora snarled. She drew a breath, her voice turning all business. "You girls have buckets to scrub," she said, and strode out of the barn.

Ana caught Rebecca's eye and motioned that they should do as they were told. As they gathered buckets, brushes, and stools to sit on as they worked, Rebecca tried to collect her thoughts. Since Flora wasn't going to admit she had poisoned Ollie's milk, the first step in proving her guilt would be to find evidence before Flora had a chance to hide it. If Flora had poisoned Ollie, then there probably would be rat poison right here in the barn, near the milk.

Swiftly, before Flora could return, Rebecca explained her thinking to Ana. "Will you help me search?" Rebecca pleaded.

Ana's voice was soft but resolute. "I will help," she said. "But only to show you are wrong about Flora."

Together, Rebecca and Ana began peering into corners, barrels, and cupboards for anything labeled "RAT POISON." Nothing. Almost bursting with frustration, Rebecca carried the buckets and cleaning supplies outside. As she set them down, another idea came to her.

She called to Flora, who was walking past the barn toward the cottages. "There are only a few drops of bleach left," Rebecca said, lifting the bleach jug and shaking it as proof. "Where can I find more?"

"The storage room's in the basement," Flora answered. She sighed and looked to Ana. "The jugs are heavy when they're full, and we'll need more than one. Go with her, but make it quick."

Grabbing Ana's hand, Rebecca dashed down the stairs, ignoring the scuttling shadows on the landing and the echoing *slap-slap* of their rubber boots on the steps. They reached the lobby level and continued down the poorly lit staircase to the basement. The light grew dimmer with every step, and a dank odor rose around them.

"I do not like this," Ana said.

"Me neither," Rebecca answered.

By the time they were on the last step, the stairwell was so dark that Rebecca put her hands out in front of her to feel what lay ahead. A door. A knob. She turned it and stepped through.

Musty air engulfed the girls. Rebecca found a light, but it scarcely lit a circle a few feet in diameter. A few small windows near the ceiling let in narrow shafts of light—just enough to reveal lumps and strange shapes lining an open aisle. As Rebecca's

eyes adjusted, she picked her way through racks
of costumes and enough props to fill several apart-
ments—lamps, tables, a rocking chair, a dining table.

Just as she was passing a sofa, something suddenly
seemed to lunge out at her. Its eyes were bright, and its
wide mouth was full of teeth.

Rebecca jumped. Ana screamed.

After several long moments, the animal remained
motionless. Rebecca drew a deep breath and moved
closer. It was a real lion, stuffed by a taxidermist into
a frozen, silent roar.

Laughing weakly, the girls moved on, past
a half-dozen large Chinese paper umbrellas, a
stormy backdrop painted with menacing clouds
and lightning bolts, stacks of extra theater seats,
rolled carpets, steel pipes, cement blocks, ropes,
cables, and lumber. Everything a theater needed.
Had this been any other day, Rebecca would have
savored every detail. But she was on a mission, and
there was no time to spare.

She pointed to a door. "That has to be a storage room," she said.

The door was shut, but an open lock dangled from its metal clasp. Rebecca pushed on the door, and it swung open into blackness.

Rebecca felt around for a light switch. Nothing. How were they going to find rat poison if they couldn't see? The stale air mixed with sharp smells of turpentine, oil, and paint. Rebecca stepped into the darkness, swinging her arm ahead of her in hopes of touching a pull cord for a light. When something brushed her hands—*a spider web?*—she jumped back. Then she gulped down her nerves, felt for it again, and this time gave it a yank. A single light bulb flickered on.

Shelves lined the walls, floor to ceiling, holding cans of every size and various boxes of screws and nails. One wall above a workbench displayed all sorts of tools. Nearby, rags and paintbrushes hung from nails. Tacked on the edge of one shelf was a magazine cover featuring "The Prettiest Shopgirl in New York City." Ollie gazed back at them with smiling eyes from under a halo of white flowers encircling her hair.

"I'll bet Mr. O'Hara put that up," Rebecca whispered. "He really is a fan."

Next to the jugs of bleach on a top shelf, Rebecca spotted a box with a drawing of a fat rat nibbling on a wedge of yellow cheese. There it was. What she'd both wanted to find and dreaded finding. She stretched to her tiptoes, pulled the box from the shelf, and squinted at the label in the dim light: "BINGHAM'S BEST RAT POISON."

The box felt heavy in Rebecca's hands. She shuddered. "It doesn't prove Flora is responsible," she told Ana. "But it does show that she has access to the poison. It's right here by the farm supplies. Should we take it with us?"

"She will know we took it." Ana's voice was uncertain, and Rebecca noted with relief that she was no longer leaping to Flora's defense. "Please, let's go," Ana said. "I am afraid."

Just then, the sound of heavy footsteps stilled the girls into silence. Someone was approaching the storage room.

chapter 13
An Awful Discovery

ICE WATER SURGED through Rebecca's veins. She mouthed to Ana one word: "Flora?"

Ana's eyes widened. Rebecca felt a powerful need to hide. Had the real reason they'd gone to the basement occurred to Flora? Had she followed them? If she saw them here with the rat poison, what might she do to keep them quiet?

In a rush, Rebecca shoved the box back on the shelf and looked frantically for a hiding place. In the corner, a wooden desk piled with old flyers and playbills offered a space big enough for both of them. The girls dove under the desk and pressed themselves against the cold, dusty floor. Rebecca prayed no rats were nearby.

Step by step, someone covered the distance

176

between the stairs and the storage room. The footsteps drew closer and stopped.

"Sure'n someone's left things open wide as the sky," came Mr. O'Hara's singsong voice.

Rebecca felt a rush of relief, but something compelled her to stay put. "It's *not* Flora," she mouthed silently to Ana.

Ana nodded. "Should we go?" she mouthed back.

Rebecca pressed her lips together and shook her head. How would they explain hiding in the storage room if they were to crawl out now? Mr. O'Hara and Flora were friends. He would certainly need more evidence than Rebecca had to convince him of Flora's guilt.

The girls watched silently as Mr. O'Hara entered the storage room and closed the door behind him; then he withdrew a pair of black gloves from his pocket. He pulled on the gloves and reached to the top shelf for the rat poison, which he set on his workbench.

That's odd, Rebecca thought. Then she remembered that Mr. O'Hara painted and constructed scenery in the dark spaces behind the stage, the kind of spots rats seemed to love. No doubt he had frequent use for the poison.

Then Mr. O'Hara removed the metal flask from his shirt pocket.

So this is where he sneaks his drinks, Rebecca thought.

But after tugging the cork from the flask, Mr. O'Hara didn't sip from it. Instead, with the tip of a screwdriver, he withdrew a bit of the powder from the box of poison and added it carefully to his flask. Then he pushed the cork back in the flask and shook it.

As Mr. O'Hara tucked the flask back in his pocket, Rebecca recalled the way he had shooed away the baby goat that tried to lap up the liquid in the theater. What had he said? That the little goat would be sorry if he drank it.

Rebecca's heart nearly stopped. *No. He couldn't possibly . . .*

He *adores* Ollie.

Rebecca gripped Ana's hand. Nothing was making sense.

What reason could Mr. O'Hara possibly have for hurting Ollie? Could it be, as Ana had argued, that Mr. Hammerstein was forcing Mr. O'Hara into sabotaging Ollie's act? Was Mr. O'Hara doing it to keep his job?

Rebecca looked past Mr. O'Hara to the wall of tools. On a nail next to a pair of pliers hung a wire cutter. She pictured the partially severed cable of the stage swing . . . and remembered a man watching from behind the curtains with the two dancers that day. Rebecca recalled how, at the very moment Ollie fell, Mr. O'Hara was there like a knight in shining armor . . . or at least he'd seemed like one.

Suddenly things made sense in a different—and awful—way.

The source of arsenic . . . right here where Mr. O'Hara had easy access. By hiding the poison in his flask, he could easily have added a drop or two to Ollie's daily glass of milk. Flora had asked him to take milk to Ollie on Monday, when the girls were busy at Central Park buying the goats. He might have poisoned the milk then. He could have come back and poisoned it again the next day, the day the cable snapped ... and Wednesday, too. The next day, Thursday, Ollie had gotten sick.

Rebecca realized that she had been completely wrong about Flora! It had been Mr. O'Hara all along. The only thing she couldn't understand was ... why?

Suddenly Mr. O'Hara stopped moving.

Rebecca braced herself, sure he had heard them under the desk.

"Down this way," came Flora's voice from somewhere beyond the storage room door.

Flora? What on earth was going on? Could she and Mr. O'Hara be working together somehow?

In a whir of motion, Mr. O'Hara placed the rat poison back on the shelf and pulled the string to turn off the light. Then, whistling a tune, he stepped out of the storage room and closed the door.

The tiny room was utterly dark. A *clunk* echoed against its walls and left Rebecca with a dreadful feeling. Mr. O'Hara had fastened the lock behind him.

She and Ana were trapped.

chapter 14
Trapped

REBECCA STIFLED THE urge to shout for help. She strained to hear what was happening outside the door. "Mr. O'Hara," Flora was saying, "I just sent Beckie and Ana down here to get some bleach. Have you seen them?"

"Sorry, no," Mr. O'Hara replied. "Is something wrong?"

"Very wrong," said Flora. "Someone has used arsenic to poison a couple of the dancers over at the New Amsterdam. We have reason to believe the girls are involved."

Rebecca's chest heaved. Was Flora linking Rebecca and Ana to the crime to take suspicion off herself? And who was the "we" Flora was speaking of?

"That so?" asked Mr. O'Hara.

"One of the girls gave Tilly Parker a glass of milk to drink earlier today." This voice belonged to another man. "Miss Parker said the girl snatched the glass away and told her it contained poison."

The man's words hit Rebecca like a blow. She hadn't *really* wanted Tilly to drink the milk. Now everyone thought Rebecca was guilty. Maybe even Ollie thought so!

"I would never have guessed, officer," Mr. O'Hara said. "They seemed like good girls."

At the word *officer*, the girls gasped.

"Flora brought police!" Ana whispered. "We can explain to officer?"

"It's worth the risk," Rebecca whispered back. "Officer, help!" she yelled at the top of her lungs. "We're here!"

"Help!" Ana joined in. "Help!"

"Unlock that door!" the officer commanded.

"Sure thing, officer," said Mr. O'Hara. "I thought I was alone in there. I'm telling ye true."

There was the rattle of keys and the thump of the door being pushed open abruptly. A light flickered on. "Girls! Where are ye now?" Mr. O'Hara called. He stepped right in front of the desk where Rebecca and Ana hid.

From under the table, Rebecca waited until Mr. O'Hara's worn work boots, splattered with dried paint, were joined by a larger pair of shiny black shoes and Flora's smaller rubber boots. Then Rebecca and Ana scooted out from under the desk and stood up.

"Oh!" Mr. O'Hara said under his breath, as if two ghosts had appeared before him out of thin air. He looked to the officer and, as if to implicate the girls, pointed to the shelf. "That's rat poison right behind 'em. It's full of arsenic."

"Right," said the officer. Blocking the doorway, his head nearly touching the top of the door frame, he gazed down at the girls.

Rebecca didn't wait for his questions. Hands

trembling, voice shaking, she told the officer as much as she could in a single breath: how they came down for bleach and ended up seeing Mr. O'Hara put rat poison into his metal flask, the one he always carried in his pocket.

"Oh, don't go on like that," Mr. O'Hara said, waving his hand as if batting away a fly. Tiny droplets of sweat beaded up on his sunburned forehead. "She is just a wee child."

The officer held up his hand. "Let's hear her out."

Rebecca went on. She told the officer about how Ollie's swing had been tampered with and pointed to the wall of tools. "He has wire cutters—there."

"I am a craftsman," Mr. O'Hara protested. "I use tools. 'Tis nothing wrong with that."

"You were there the very moment she fell from the broken swing," Rebecca said, challenging him.

"A lucky thing, that," Mr. O'Hara countered. "If me friend hadn't let me in to see the rehearsals, I'd not have been there to catch her."

Rebecca pressed on, explaining to the officer how she hadn't intended for Tilly Parker to drink the milk. "She was so envious of Miss Berry. I—I was convinced she was the one who had added the arsenic," Rebecca explained, feeling foolish. "If Tilly had poisoned the milk, I knew she wouldn't drink it, so I gave Tilly the glass as a test. She drank it before I could stop her." Rebecca hung her head. "I hope she didn't get sick."

"No," the officer said. "If there was poison in the milk, she didn't drink enough to get sick. But you sure did scare her."

"I'm very sorry." Rebecca let out a small sigh and went on. "But I've been worried to death about Ollie. I knew someone wished her harm, but I didn't know who—until now."

She turned to Mr. O'Hara. "But why? How could you hurt someone you love? I suppose the poetry was all an act. And all the ways you were trying to help her—those were an act, too."

Mr. O'Hara's eyes softened. "'Twas no act," he said, his tone plaintive now. "I love her more than the sun, stars, and sky! I never meant to hurt her, only to ruin her show." He looked from face to face. "Just to have her back."

"Back?" Rebecca was more confused than ever.

Mr. O'Hara closed his eyes, as if remembering something painful. "I know the *real* Ollie," he said. "Back when she was Olivia Kelly and the only songs she sang were Irish ones. On the ship from Ireland, she was a small lamb of six and I was ten. I kept her from cryin' with me jokes and poetry." He shook his head. "But our journey didn't end there. Our families landed in the same little town in Pennsylvania, and as we grew older, we grew sweet on each other, we did." He paused and smiled softly. But after a moment, the smile faded. "And then one day she up and left. I picked up the newspaper a year later and saw the face of the 'Prettiest Shopgirl in New York City.' When she showed up at the Follies, I found a job here, hoping that we could start anew."

Rebecca almost felt sorry for him. But his story still didn't explain why he thought he needed to get Ollie off the stage. She waited patiently for him to continue.

"And on Monday, when I delivered the milk to her, I saw me chance. I asked her to marry me." He sighed and lowered his gaze to the floor. "But she'd have none of it. Stagestruck, she is." He stared past them and his face grew dark.

Rebecca inched closer to Flora and Ana.

Mr. O'Hara continued. "She'd fallen under Mr. Ziegfeld's spell. All this time, I'd been pinin' for her, but at least I had hope—until Monday. She said that after the new show, there'd be no stoppin' her. If it were a hit, she'd be a Broadway star, and I knew she'd never have me. I felt desperate. Time was running out."

He looked from Flora to the officer. "I used just a wee bit of the powder the past few days. Just the smallest pinch to keep her off that stage. Mr. Ziegfeld would let her go then, and she'd give up on these silly dreams and fall back in me arms."

The officer presented a set of handcuffs. "Mr. O'Hara, you're under arrest."

Mr. O'Hara didn't resist as the officer snapped the handcuffs shut. Hands bound, he slumped.

Rebecca felt more angry now than afraid. "You cut the wire on Ollie's swing. She could have broken her neck!"

Mr. O'Hara shook his head. "I meant only to give her a fright." He glanced around, as if pleading his case to a jury. "I was there to catch her. You saw that," he said to Rebecca.

"All I saw," Rebecca said hotly, "was someone trying to look like a hero. Someone who is just the opposite."

"Nay, the only thing I'm guilty of—I tell ye true—is love." He closed his eyes and recited in a melodious voice:

"Sure as stars in the heavens,
You and I are joined,
my bonnie love,
by silvery cords to the mast of a golden ship . . ."

"That's enough," the officer said. "Let's get you to the station."

The moment the officer led Mr. O'Hara away, Ana threw her arms around Flora's waist. "I'm sorry!" she cried. "I was wrong to doubt you!"

Rebecca kept her feet planted on the cool basement floor. "I'm sorry, too," she said.

Flora let out a deep breath. "Come along," she said. "My customers will be coming soon. We can talk as we head back upstairs."

As they climbed the steps, Rebecca apologized again. "Given your history, I'm sure you have your reasons to be upset with Ollie," she continued. "But when you said 'she deserves it,' I was certain you were involved."

"Girls," Flora said, stopping midstep, "I should never have said that—or many of the mean things I've said about Ollie. No wonder you thought it could be me. You were only trying to protect her. My words have all been about lashing out at her. I'm the one who's sorry. I was just so upset about her stealing Frank away that I ..." she trailed off as she continued up the steps.

Rebecca cast a meaningful glance back at Ana on the stairs before she spoke again. "Flora, there's something I was afraid to tell you before," Rebecca said. "And now I can." She stopped on the landing and waited for Flora to face her. "Frank sent roses and a love note to Ollie. We saw it in her dressing room. It was signed just the way he signed his last note to you. But Ollie wasn't even interested enough to read it. I can assure you that she only has eyes for Mr. Ziegfeld."

Rebecca exhaled. *There. It was out.*

"I am sorry, Flora," Ana said, taking her hand.

"Your fiancé Frank, he is not good man."

Flora looked upward, into the distance, as if she were trying to see straight through the walls of the stairwell to the sky outside. "Thank you, girls, for being honest. The truth is, I think I already knew that. I had a good long talk with myself about his last note, and I started to wonder if I was angry at the wrong person."

There was a brief silence.

"Do you still want us to scrub buckets today?" Ana asked finally.

Flora shook her head with a gentle smile. "Let's save that for tomorrow. It's Friday, and I think you both need a little rest. Head on home now. If you stop by Mr. Hammerstein's office on your way out, his secretary should have your pay."

Then she reached into a pocket in her apron and pulled out an envelope. "And before you go, I want you girls to deliver this to Frank. I've been debating about whether to give it to him. But after what you've just told me, I'm certain."

A doubtful look crossed Ana's face. She took the envelope by one corner.

"It's not what you think," Flora said, smiling. "It's definitely *not* a love letter. Sometimes, a girl's just got to take a stand." As they climbed the last flight of stairs, Flora's step seemed somehow lighter.

chapter 15

Opening Night

THE GIRLS GATHERED their belongings, bid Flora good-bye, and headed back down the stairs toward Mr. Hammerstein's office. Two steps before the lobby level, Rebecca froze, pulling Ana back. "Oh!" Her voice caught in her throat.

On the floor just in front of the stairwell door, a small rat looked up from a half-eaten bread roll. The girls must have startled the rat, too, because it didn't seem to know whether to keep eating the roll or flee. For a long moment, the rat stared them down.

Suddenly, Ana took a step toward the rat. She clapped her hands over her head and shouted. "Go!"

At that, the rat darted off under the landing railing and into a dark space below.

The girls hurried down the last stairs and out

through the door to the main level.

"Good job, Ana," Rebecca said. "I was so afraid that my legs wouldn't move."

Ana stood a little taller. "I was scared also, but then I decide to act big and brave. It worked!" She broke into a broad smile.

Rebecca laughed. "You were acting, Ana. See? Acting skills do come in handy sometimes."

As they found their way to Mr. Hammerstein's office, Ana's expression grew serious. "I am sorry I say some bad things about acting. I know you love this acting and theater. It is not all spying and bad people."

Rebecca stopped to face her cousin. "Thank you, Ana. I'll never give up my dreams. But you weren't wrong—not entirely. I was so fascinated by Olivia Berry and the Follies that I got mixed up. I told myself that *spying* was acting, that *lying* was acting. I feel terrible that I pulled you into all of this."

Ana gave Rebecca a big hug. "Is true that Bubbie

would not be happy if she knew of all this," Ana said with a sly grin. "But if you were bad actress, Ollie would still be in danger, and Flora would have heart broken. You deserve standing ovation. You saved the day!"

"*We* saved the day," Rebecca corrected her.

After receiving their pay envelopes and tucking them safely in their overalls, the girls left the building and crossed the street to the New Amsterdam Theater.

"Hello," Ana said, handing Flora's sealed letter to the doorman. "For you."

Frank curled one end of his mustache and studied the letter with his name on it. "Thank you, girls," he said, opening the door for them.

Rebecca and Ana stepped inside and headed toward Ollie's dressing room.

When Rebecca knocked, Ollie replied uncertainly, "Come in?"

"Beckie!" Ollie sat at her table, drawing a silver-backed brush through her shiny hair.

Rebecca entered, stopping short when she saw Tilly Parker stretched out on the chaise, her long legs crossed. She wore ruffles and high heels and held a sharp nail file in her hand.

"What do you know!" Tilly Parker exclaimed. "It's the girl who tried to poison me!"

Embarrassed, Rebecca fought the urge to run away. But she needed to tell Ollie that the culprit had been caught. And, she told herself sternly, she needed to make things right with Tilly—or try, at least.

"Hello, Miss Parker," Rebecca began. "I'm so very sorry. I lied about the milk coming from Ollie—but you probably figured that out already. I thought if you refused to drink it that it would prove you were guilty of trying to poison Ollie. But I hadn't thought what to do if you *weren't* guilty. You started drinking the milk before I could stop you. I hope you can forgive me—someday."

"The good news," Tilly said, "is that I didn't get sick. I called the doctor right away. And he called the police. The other good news is that Ollie's convinced me you meant no harm."

"Tilly and I have been piecing things together," Ollie said. "But we still can't figure out who—"

"We catch him," Ana announced.

"Who?" Ollie asked.

"Mr. O'Hara," Rebecca explained. "We saw him put rat poison in his flask, and he admitted that he's the one who poisoned your milk and tampered with the swing."

"Darby O'Hara?" Ollie's jaw dropped. She let the silver brush slip from her hand and gripped the sides of her dressing table to steady herself. "I would never have thought. He and I go back a long way. We were childhood sweethearts. Then he showed up working right across the street at the Victory. And this very Monday, out of the blue—"

"He asked you to marry him," Rebecca said.

"Yes. He wanted to take me back to our little town in Pennsylvania." Ollie's eyes were big, beautiful, and bewildered. "I couldn't imagine he was serious. How could he think I might be happier there? And how could he think hurting me would win me back?" She took up the hairbrush and brushed vigorously from the crown of her head to the ends of her locks, as if trying to rid herself of the thought.

"He believed that if he ruined your act, Mr. Ziegfeld would lose interest in you," Rebecca explained. "And if he came to your rescue, you'd fall back in love with him."

"Then he never knew me at all," Ollie said, shaking her head. "Ziggy's not what keeps me going. No other man ever will be, either. I will always find a way back onstage."

Tilly stopped filing her nails. "Your 'big sister,'" she said to Rebecca with a wink, "is made of pretty tough stuff."

"But it sure helped to have a 'little sister' on my

side," Ollie said. "Beckie, you're made of tough stuff, too. I owe you a huge thanks."

"I owe you a thank-you, too, baby doll," Tilly added.

"Me? Why?" Rebecca asked.

Tilly beamed. "Somehow, because of you—Ollie and I are becoming friends."

That evening, as the girls settled into their seats for Shabbat dinner, Rebecca wished she were settling into a seat at the New Amsterdam Theater to watch Ollie's big show. But she wished it only for a moment. She was happier to be *home*. Home, squeezed between her family and Ana's, and Bubbie and Grandpa. She'd always love the stage and acting, but never again would she confuse the bright lights and excitement with what was important in life.

After the candles were lit and the prayers were recited, Rebecca and Ana stood and presented their pay envelopes to Rebecca's aunt and uncle.

"This is such a gift," Uncle Josef said. "You girls make miracle trick!"

"You mean magic trick," Ana said, hugging her papa.

"It is miracle, too," Ana's mama added, giving each girl a kiss on the cheek.

Rebecca looked around the table at each and every face. She was surrounded by the people who knew her strengths and her shortcomings ... the people who loved her for who she truly was. Her family.

That evening, Rebecca thought the challah had never tasted sweeter, and the candles glowed more brightly than any spotlight. Basking in their glow, Rebecca made a vow to herself: Onstage or off-, whatever challenges came her way in life, she would always be her truest and best self—and treat every moment like it was opening night.

Inside Rebecca's World

During Rebecca's time, before air-conditioning helped keep things cool indoors, people flocked outside to beat the heat. In a crowded city like New York, one of the coolest places to be during a heat wave was up on a breezy rooftop. New York had many rooftop restaurants and attractions, and the one in this story is based on a real place: the Paradise Roof Gardens. Like the one in the story, the Paradise Roof Gardens were created by theater owner Oscar Hammerstein I, grandfather to the famous lyricist, Oscar Hammerstein II. He dreamed up the rooftop "farm" as a way to lure New Yorkers to his theater—and keep them away from competitors.

At the Paradise Roof Gardens, a girl of Rebecca's time might have felt like a girl of today at an amusement park. She could ride a boat on a miniature lake, see a dazzling light display, eat in a restaurant, and pet real farm animals at a minature farm. She could even enjoy a glass of milk fresh from the cows that lived in the barn year-round. For city dwellers, the cows—and the young women who milked them—were the stars of the show.

Stage shows at the rooftop garden were part of a theater tradition called vaudeville. Vaudeville shows featured a variety of short acts, including bands, comedians, jugglers, dancers, and acrobats. They also featured animal acts, such as cowboy comedian Will Rogers and his horse. In one famous vaudeville act, trained rats rode on the backs of cats, skittered across tightropes, and even carried miniature American flags!

Among the most famous of all the vaudeville shows were the Ziegfeld Follies, created by Florenz Ziegfeld. Every show featured a group of dancers known as Ziegfeld Girls, who performed in elaborate—and daring—costumes. Ziegfeld Girls, like the fictional Olivia Berry in the story, captivated audiences with their beauty and talent, and some found their way from the Follies stage to stardom in other shows and movies.

You can no longer see the Ziegfeld Follies in a theater, but you can see what they were like by watching classic movies like *Ziegfeld Follies,* starring Fred Astaire, or *Funny Girl,* starring Barbra Streisand as the real-life Ziegfeld Girl Fanny Brice. And the vaudeville tradition lives on today in another place you might not expect. Where can you go to watch a lot of short acts featuring a dizzying variety of performers all in one evening and all in one place, just as vaudeville audiences did a long time ago? Right to your TV, computer, or smartphone!

Read more of REBECCA'S stories,

available from booksellers and at *americangirl.com*

∞ *Classics* ∞

Rebecca's classic series, now in two volumes:

Volume 1:
The Sound of Applause
Rebecca uses her talents to help cousin Ana escape Russia. Now she must share everything with Ana—even the stage!

Volume 2:
Lights, Camera, Rebecca!
Rebecca gets the best birthday present ever—a role in a real movie. But she can't tell anyone in her family about it.

∞ *Journey in Time* ∞

Travel back in time—and spend a day with Rebecca.

The Glow of the Spotlight

Step inside Rebecca's world and the excitement of New York City in 1914! Bargain with street peddlers, and audition for a Broadway show. Choose your own path through this multiple-ending story.

∞ *Mysteries* ∞

Suspense and sleuthing with Rebecca.

A Growing Suspicion: A Rebecca Mystery

Who is jinxing the Japanese garden where Rebecca and Ana volunteer?

The Crystal Ball: A Rebecca Mystery

A black pigeon carries an eerie message to the coop on Rebecca's rooftop. Only a visit to a fortune-teller will reveal its meaning!

A Sneak Peek at

A Growing
Suspicion

A Rebecca Mystery

Step into another suspenseful
adventure with Rebecca!

"LETS GO BACK to the secret garden and check around," Rebecca suggested. "We have to prove that we didn't leave those footprints."

Ana kept working. "Maybe after we plant the ferns," she replied.

The cousins dug one hole after another until Rebecca's muscles ached. She stood up and rubbed her stiff neck. "Look," she said, pointing across the pond. "There's the couple that was in the sand garden yesterday." She pointed at two people on a small island, leaning against some low boulders. "I'm sure it's them," Rebecca declared. "No one else here wears such fancy clothes. How did they get out there?"

The woman on the island gestured toward some shrubs, and then Rebecca saw her pluck a blossom and tuck it into the man's lapel before they walked on.

"She picked a flower!" Rebecca fumed. "Miss Ward told us not to take even a dead leaf! Those two act as if they own the place, but I'll bet they're up to no good. I think we should find out what's going on."

"We'd better not," Ana protested. But Rebecca strode down the path that wound around the pond, pulling Ana along.

"We should keep working," Ana said, trying to turn back. "The holes are almost done, and we can plant the ferns lickety-split."

"But this could be our only chance to investigate," Rebecca said. "If they left footprints behind, we can go back to the sand garden and see if they match. Then we'd know they were the ones who messed it up." She held Ana's hand firmly and circled around the pond.

"We really have to get back to the fern garden," Ana said, pulling her hand free, "before you get us into hot water." She tapped a bamboo railing that blocked the bank leading from the pathway to the pond. "Anyway, there's no way down."

"That couple got down there somehow," Rebecca mused. She walked a bit farther, looking for an opening in the low fence. "There!" She pointed to a steep path that led to a bridge. The narrow bamboo bridge arched over a stream that separated the main garden from the tiny island. Without hesitating, Rebecca tripped down the path and carefully crossed the bridge.

Rebecca stepped onto the island and began searching the ground for footprints. Instead of a sandy bank, smooth stones and pebbles rolled under her feet. The bank was too stony for footprints.

"Come back," Ana called down to her. "Please, Beckie!"

Rebecca waved gaily to her cousin and moved closer to the island's edge, hoping to find soft sand there. Instead, she discovered a curving line of large round stepping-stones that led across the water and toward two tall, unmoving birds. The birds were made of bronze, yet they seemed so lifelike, Rebecca almost expected them to fly away. Everything was so intriguing that all thoughts of finding out about the mysterious couple disappeared from Rebecca's head.

"Watch this, Ana," she shouted as she hopped onto the first stone. She did a pirouette on the flat stone, feeling it wobble slightly as she twirled. She glanced up and saw Ana smile.

Feeling encouraged, Rebecca danced from one stone to the next, farther and farther from shore. Then, in the midst of a one-legged spin, her arms outstretched, Rebecca was startled by a shout from the bridge above her.

"Come up here at once, young lady!" Miss Ward and her class appeared on the wide wooden bridge high above the pond. Her face darkened.

Rebecca jumped back across the stones in a panic. Miss Ward would be furious—and worse, Ana would be, too.

Just as Rebecca landed with two feet on the stepping-stone closest to shore, it teetered, throwing her off balance—and Rebecca stumbled into the pond with a splash.

About the Author

MARY CASANOVA is the author of numerous books for American Girl. To write this mystery, she criss-crossed New York City for research and took in a few Broadway shows, including the opening night of a show her son helped produce. When she's not writing—or traveling to speak at schools and conferences—she's likely to be reading a good book, horseback riding, or hiking with her husband, three dogs, and—on occasion—their two adventurous cats in the north woods of Minnesota.